Onesimus,
The Run-Away Slave

By

Ernest A. Jones SR

ISBN: 1-4140-3694-9 (e-book)
ISBN: 1-4140-3693-0 (Paperback)

This book is printed on acid free paper.

1stBooks - rev. 02/04/04

CHAPTER 1

He wrinkled his brow as he tried to remember what he had heard the night before. Placing his arms behind his neck he leaned back against the old gnarled sycamore-fig tree and stared up through its dense layer of green leaves. "What was it," he said outloud as he tried to remember. Thinking he was asleep on his mat in the back corner of the room, his parents had talked quietly in the night. "What had father said?"

"Oh yes, now I remember, they were talking about our neighbors, the ones who lived just a 15 minute walk from our house. Our neighbors place was raided. All their sheep and cattle were stolen and their small daughter was kidnapped too. She was just about my age and very pretty. Will I ever get to see her again?" he wondered outloud. He shivered even though it was warm out.

"Omne, Omne, Where are you? Omne, Omne," the anxious voice rolled over the land.

Terror gripped the boy's soul as he started to run to the voice. "I'm coming mother! I am right here! What do you want?"

"Oh there you are. Where were you? I was so afraid something had happened to you. Why didn't you answer me sooner?" The woman's face was wreathed in worry wrinkles, her eyes dark with fear as her small son drew near.

"I am sorry mother. I guess I was thinking and didn't hear you. But why were you afraid for me? I will not get hurt here.

Why, how could any harm come to me here?"

"I had better tell you. We did not want to worry you and so planned not to say anything to you. But now I see I must tell you, but I don't want the little ones hearing about this. They will be too frightened if they hear this horrible news. Do not tell them"

"I won't mother if you don't want me to tell them"

His mother took in a deep breath and continued, her voice now quiet and soft. "Yesterday a band of raiders raided our neighbors place. They stole all their sheep and cattle. And they stole their small daughter. The girl's father and older brothers and sisters were away at the time. Now the little girl will become a slave if she can't be found soon."

"They took my friend Mary didn't they?" He searched her face for hope but saw only fear in her eyes.

Yes, they took her. How did you know?"

"Last night I heard you and father talking."

"So you already knew?"

"Yes, I was just out under my favorite tree thinking about what I had heard."

"Now you will understand why I became afraid when you did not answer right away; I was afraid that the raiders had returned and taken you. Please be very careful and stay close by."

"I will mother. I will be very careful and stay close. I don't want to be stolen away. Do you think they will come back tonight?"

"Now don't be scared. I do not think they will return tonight or soon for they will know that everyone here will be on the look out for them. No they won't return soon, she added almost as a plea. As long as you stay close to the house you will be safe. Your father will do all he can to protect us. And we will never leave you here alone. We

2

will pray to our god and he will help us. You know he is strong."

"Yes I know that. But how can he help us. He can't even move. Why all he can do is sit in that corner. Really he scares me."

"Son! You must never talk that way! He will be angry at us! He will help us, you will see."

"Well the neighbor's god did not help them. Is our god stronger than their god?"

"Oh yes, son, our god is the strongest. Their god was made of wood. Ours is made out of silver, pure silver. He is the strongest god there is."

"Mother, Samuel says that his God is stronger than ours.

Is that true. If so why don't we worship his God?"

"I don't think his God is anything at all. Why you can't even see his god. We can see our god."

"Okay mother," he answered. But as he turned away he muttered to himself; "sure we can see our god. He sits in that dark corner all the time and never moves or speaks. He is ugly. I hate him." With that he returned to his favorite tree and sat where he could see down the road. He would watch for the raiders. They would never capture him.

In the house his mother worried over her first born son. He was a good son, never causing any trouble. But his attitude about their god worried her. Maybe their god would get angry with them. Maybe trouble would come to them. So she brooded over this problem and wondered how to help her young son to love their god.

Years went by and the family continued to grow. Now the boy had 3 sisters and 3 brothers. He helped his father work in the fields. All day they would work. It was hard but the boy did not complain. He liked the work and especially liked to drive the team of oxen as they plowed the land. He was now nearly a man.

He was handsome and very strong and could do nearly as much work as his father. He had almost forgotten that day long ago when his neighbor's

little girl was kidnapped. Her family never saw
her again. He still wondered about his god and he
still thought his god was worthless. But he never
talked about this to anyone. He was afraid that
something bad would happen to him. He did not love
his god; one might even say that he despised the
ugly silver god that always stared angrily at him.

The day Omne turned 14 years old his father came
home with another team of oxen. Both of these
large animals were white with long horns. His
father had been assured that they were very gentle
and were dependable working oxen.

Omne hurried to his father, excitement shining
in his eyes. "Father, where did you get them? Are
you going to sell our old pair?"

His father smiled at his first born son. How he
loved this boy and now his eyes sparkled as he
spoke. "My son, these are for you. I think you
are now old enough to have your own oxen so I
bought these for you. With your own team we can
work together and finish our work sooner. We can
now plant that other field too. Do you like them?"

"Yes I like them, and the boy walked up to the
animals and patted their broad sides. The oxen
looked at him with their large brown eyes and
slowly chewed their cud.

From that day on, father and son would work
their own teams and the land's production increased
greatly.

The new team proved to indeed be gentle and
would respond willingly to the boy's soft but firm
command.

Then one day as Omne was plowing alone with his
team of oxen, he saw a group of men coming down the
road. There were 5 men. He was sure he didn't
know them. The men turned off the dusty road and
started across the newly plowed field towards him.
Omne watched them approach him and wondered where
they came from. He started to walk towards them
when a sudden jab of fear stabbed his heart.
Standing beside the oxen he stood still as he
watched the men. Suddenly he knew that the men

were not friendly. How had they known he was alone
that day? Actually as the men surrounded him he
was glad he was alone for if his father had been
home he might have been killed. If his younger
brothers and sisters were home they might be taken
too. Frantically he looked for a hiding place but
there were none. He was totally alone in the
middle of this large field and he felt a stab of
fear surge through his whole being, a fear he had
never known before. Quickly his eyes scanned the
land for a way of escape but there was none.

Knowing he was no match for so many men he tried
to appear calm. He greeted them with friendliness,
"Well now, What can I do for you men? Can I get
you a cool drink of water? It is warm out today
and you must be thirsty." Smiling he looked at
them.

"Stop the babbel," the leader of the group
snarled. "you are going with us." His eyes were
dark while an angry look covered his unshaved dirty
face.

"Aren't you making a mistake. Why take me?
What can I do for you?" Omne tried not to show the
fear that gripped his very soul. He studied the
men; they were a dirty lot. All wore filthy
clothes and Omne could smell the foul odor flowing
out from them. Several of the men had jagged scars
on their faces and hands. No one smiled but all
showed an evil intent.

With a sneer one of the men answered him. "What
can you do for us? You will see. Now come with us
or it will be worse for you."

Omne turned towards his house and thinking he
could scare the men, he called loudly, "Father,
Uncle Dan, I need your help now."

The words were hardly out of his mouth before a
filthy hand slapped him across his mouth. The hand
held firmly, nearly smothering him with its tight
grip. Suddenly the hand gave a mighty shove and
Omne was flung to the ground. Immediately he was
given a hard kick to his thigh and almost as

quickly jerked again to his feet. "No more of that noise," one of the men cursed. We already know you are alone here. It won't do you any good to call for help." With that two of the men grabbed him and tied his arms tightly behind his back. He was then chained between two of the men and they hurried down the road.

Hour after hour he was pushed along. His thigh hurt and often sharp pains radiated throughout his leg.

All day they walked and when night came they slept in the brush. He was so tired. He had been given no food all day, not even a swallow of water. Now as he was at last allowed to sit down, he was near collapse. Roughly he was tied to a scrubby tree and left alone.

"Where are they taking me? What will happen to me?" he wondered. He tried to pray to his god but how could he pray to him when he could not see him? "My god is probably angry with me and this is why I was captured and dragged away." He longed to rub his sore thigh or his sore wrists but his hands were still tied and he could not even give himself this little relief.

He thought about his family. "Would they know what had happened? This was only the second time that his father had left him home alone while he took the rest of the family to town with him. Omne knew the oxen would stand in the spot they had been left in and not move until instructed to move. Somehow he thought it was all his fault and he was more concerned for his family than for himself. It was as though he had let them down. "Yes, my family knows. Father would have seen all the tracks around where the oxen stood. Maybe right now help is on the way. Maybe I should yell out for help; then they might hear me. No," he reasoned to himself, "That will only get me in more trouble; maybe these men will even kill me if I do that. Oh," he moaned quietly to himself, "I am so tired and thirsty." His stomach growled as if in response to his thoughts.

He had just closed his eyes when he felt a slight kick to his left thigh. Startled he looked up. A man was standing over him with a goatskin. It looked like the goatskin was full. Could it be water?

"Here," the man said. "Drink this." There was a slight look of pity in the man's face. With a start Omne noted that this man was but a boy himself, probably not much older than he.

Taking the goatskin he said, "thank you. I am so thirsty." He took a long drink of the water. It was warm and did not taste near as good as the cool water from the deep well at home but it was water and quenched his thirst.

He took several long drinks before the other boy took the goatskin away. He was revived some, maybe he would live after all.

Lying on the rough, stony ground Omne tried to relax his taunt muscles and hoped for sleep to put an end to this terrible nightmare. His whole body ached and again his stomach growled with hunger. He tried to change his position but the short chains made moving very difficult. He thought of home and knew complete loneliness and fear.

CHAPTER 2

He slept fitfully that night, for though Omne was not a small boy now, he was still very homesick. He cried softly often during the night. He tried to be brave but as he was not yet 15 years old it was hard to be brave. He knew it would be better for him if he didn't fight his captors, but his whole being pleaded for him to try to flee. "But even if I could get away I have no idea where I am; how would I find home?" He turned slowly so he could look up at the stars and was surprised to see they looked just like they did at home. The night was clear and though he was glad it was not raining, he still shivered in the cool of the night. He had been given no covers to keep him warm. Then after all the other men had gone to sleep Amil, for that was the young man's name, brought a goats skin and covered Omne with it. Though no words were spoken, Omne felt a kinship with this lad. He wondered why such a lad was with this rough group. But for now he was too tired, to homesick, to alone to care about another. He tried to sit up but could not as the chains were too short. All he could do was turn from one side to the other. The ground was hard and there were rough rocks under him. They seemed to cut into his very soul. What were these men going to do with him? He had heard of men like this. Would they abuse him?

Would they make him be a slave to their every wish? Or would they carry him far away and sell him in another land as a slave there. His family did not have any slaves. They had some servants which were treated like family. But he had heard how slaves were treated. He shivered now more from fear than the cold. Omne tried to sleep but would just drift off to sleep when he would suddenly jerk wide awake. "Oh mother, oh father," he cried silently to himself. "What is going to happen to me? Will you find me soon? Will I ever see you again?"

The Eastern sky was just showing a hint of light when the men got up. Everyone ignored Omne, just as if he were not even there, while they hurried to break camp. Finally Amil came and untied him. He led him away from camp for a few minutes. Omne was glad for this. Amil spoke little, as if he were afraid he might be heard by the others. But once he whispered ever so quietly, "you must cooperate if you want to live. Some of the men are watching you and you could be harmed. The leader thinks you will be worth much money and no one will harm you as long as you behave yourself well. But if you do not, there will be no protection for you. Do you understand what I am saying?"

"Yes."

"Amil, where are you?" Loud, angry voices sounded in the early morning air.

"Ready? We must go back now."

Entering the camp, one man told Amil to hurry and get the food ready to eat. Amil hurried but was not fast enough for the man. The man slapped Amil hard across his back, nearly sending the young man to the ground.

A surge of anger flooded throughout Omne as he observed this harsh treatment. "I would help him if I could, but I am chained," he mumbled quietly to himself. Fear mixed with anger flashed in his eyes. Then as Omne looked at Amil, there eyes met for just an instant, but it was long enough for Omne to understand. He knew Amil was with them not because he wanted to be with them, but he was also a slave. It was now that Omne noted the bruises on Amil's face and arms. "Well," he thought to himself, "If I ever get away from these men I will also see that Amil goes with me."

Breakfast was nothing more than some cold meat and dried bread. There was water to drink and after the cool of the night it tasted better. They started on there way as soon as their meal was finished.

Again Omne was chained between two of the men, the same two men who were always watching him. Their evil looks worried him. He tried to ignore their talk as they hurried along but he heard enough to cause fear in his heart. He wondered if the boss would be able to protect him after all. "Well there is one thing for sure, I can not get away from them now. But I will escape! I will find a way soon."

The land was dreary and desolate. They appeared to be in the most barren land. He saw no other dwellings and they met no other people. "It is no wonder," he reasoned, "this is not much more then a wild animal trail we are following. Probably no one lives anywhere near here." The only water was the little they carried with them and this was nearly gone. The day grew extremely hot and Omne missed his hat. He remembered he had been wearing a hat, the new one his mother had just made for him, when he was captured. He wondered what had happened to it. Taking his eyes off the trail Omne looked around him. Then he stumbled and nearly pulled the two men down on him. With loud cursing the men caught Omne and stopped his fall. "Watch where you are going. You might get hurt. Good thing we caught you and one of the men kicked Omne hard. Say, you're sure a good looking lad. How old are you?"

Omne was angry at himself for stumbling but became more upset over the men's remarks. He remained quiet and did not answer hoping the men would forget. He relaxed a little when he heard the men talking about other things. One thing they said that Omne heard was that they were to be home by dark. "Where is that?" Omne wondered. He was so tired of walking. It was the most desolate land he had ever thought existed.

His whole being felt near collapse. His body was covered with dust from the trail and rivulets of sweat trickled down his face and back.

Every sinew ached and fear grew in his heart. He was faint from hunger and his mouth and throat was parched from the heat and lack of water.

Dusk was settling over the land when Omne realized they were entering a small village. Even in the growing darkness Omne could tell it was one of the dirtiest villages he had ever seen. Filth and waste was everywhere. Chickens were just now going to roost in the low scrub trees and also on the porches and roof tops. Pigs were all over the place. Garbage was scattered around and the whole place stunk.

Women, children and old men streamed out of the huts to meet them. In the confusion Omne was forgotten for awhile. He was so weary and tired. He yearned for his home and clean bed. The two men had tied him to one of the scrub trees and apparently forgotten him. Then he felt someone at his side.

"Here, come with me. I will show you where you can sleep for the night. Amil untied him and the two walked a short distance to a tent. It was made out of goat skins and was small, just long enough for a man to stretch out in. Omne noted there were two sleeping pads. Fear was on his face as he asked. "Who else will sleep in here?"

"I Will. Do not be afraid of me. You are safe for the night."

The two young men settled down on their mats As the village quieted in the growing darkness.

The night was growing cold and Omne was glad that there were skins to cover him. Even though

11

the bed was not very clean, at least he was able to get warm.

Quietly he asked, "Amil, why are you here? Did they capture you too? How long have you been here? How old are you?"

"I am 16 years old and have been here 5 years. Yes they captured me too but they killed all of my family. I had run away and hid from them but one of the men found me. I came from a little town not far from where you lived. I stay with them as there is no place else for me to go. Usually I am well cared for. Some of the men are not good to me but most treat me well."

"Sure they do. I saw that man slap you. He had no right to hit you like that. Also you have bruises all over you, and still you say they treat you well?"

"Yes I get hit often by some of the men. But not all of them are so mean. Still what else is there for me to do?"

"We could run away. Go with me and we will go to my home."

"We can't do that Omne. They would come and get us. They would treat us very bad then and they would probably kill all your family too. No, we can not flee to your place. It would not be safe. Stay here with me for awhile. You will be safe. Follow my instruction and no one will harm you. I am sure you will not be here long though. I heard the men talking about selling you. Really that is why they took you. They figure you are strong and will bring a good price in the market."

"Sell me? To whom?"

"Oh just anybody who will pay the price they are asking."

"If they want to sell me why don't they sell you?"

"I don't know for sure. Some how they seem to like me enough to keep me. Yet there are times I wish they would sell me. Those two that guarded you scare me. So far they have not harmed me though I often see them staring at me with that evil look in their eyes. I think they are afraid of the head man or I surely would be abused often. I watch carefully all the time, making sure I am never alone with either of them. So far I have succeeded but it is a constant worry. I do feel a little safer with you here."

"Do the people here grow their food? Are there any sheep and cattle?"

"Some of the women do have small gardens, but they keep no livestock other than pigs and chickens."

"Where do they get their meat?"

"Oh, there are the pigs and chickens plus other livestock. They steal sheep, goats and cattle for eating. When these are gone, some of the men go and steal more."

They grew quiet and before long Amil was asleep. Omne was so tired but his thoughts continued to plague him. Then, at last, he too fell asleep.

It was still dark when Amil awakened him. "We must get up. We need to go to the well and draw water for the people.

If there is not enough water when they get up we may get whipped."

"Have you been whipped?"

"Only once. That was enough. Now I get up in time so all the water is ready before they get up."

The two young men had just finished filling the last water jug and had found some wood for a fire when the people awoke. Omne was surprised at how many children there were. Amil pointed out to Omne that the older boys might not be very good to him. "Try to stay away from them for a few days. It will be better. But if they think you are afraid of them they will treat you all the worse."

Day followed day and Omne soon was used to the life in the village. At first the older boys teased Omne and when he remained quiet would start fights with him. Omne was no coward and knew how to defend himself and soon the other boys decided it was better to leave him alone.

The village was in a small valley completely surrounded by mountains. It was most desolate. Not enough vegetation grew to feed much livestock. Rocks of every size were strewn over the ground. Only a very few scrub trees grew there. Even the hills around them were bare. Always there were fighting and cursing.

The people were dirty and their clothes were filthy. Most of their clothes were very simple garments but some of the clothes were extra nice and Omne wondered where the folk got them. "Probably stolen too," he told himself.

One day, after many months, Omne heard that some men were going on another trip. He was to go also and he noted the sad look on Amil's face. "What is the matter Amil? You look so worried."

"They are taking you away. I don't know where. I was hoping they would keep you here with us. You are the only one I can talk to. You are my friend. I am scared for you to go and I don't want to be alone again either for I feel safer with you here. I fear you will be mis-treated too."

"Amil, I have been wondering for a long time about something you said. One day I asked you why you did not get angry. Why you were always so obedient. You spoke of your god. But I have never seen your god. Where is he? We had gods at home too, but they were ugly and I was afraid of them."

"My God is alive. He lives up in the heavens. He is the only true God there is. I should have told you about him sooner. Now it is too late. But remember, there is a God who lives in the heavens Who is all wise. He will listen to you. I talk to Him all the time when I am alone. He is my source of strength. I don't think I could live without Him. If you are in danger He will help you too if you call upon Him."

"Then why are you here? If He could help you why was your family killed and you made a slave here?"

"I don't have the answers for you. He has a reason but just what I do not know now. But I will still trust in Him. I hope some day you will know Him too. I will pray that you will find Him. I am sorry I never told you sooner. Here they come now. Good by my friend. My God will go with you."

"Come Omne, let us be on our way." As they started out Omne turned to face Amil one more time. Amil was standing straight and tall a smile on his face. But Omne was sure he spotted tears in his eyes. "Good by Amil" and turning, he went with the men. "Where are we going? Now what will happen to me? What about Amil's God? Who is He? Can He help me or would He want to?" Omne wondered. "I could sure use a friend now. If there is a God up there like Amil thinks, well if You are there will You help me? Will You be my Friend? I am again all alone and so scared."

"Hey Omne, hurry up. We have a long way to go today."

CHAPTER 3

It was a long and tiring day. The men pushed on with the determination and speed of one being pursued, pushing their captive to near exhaustion. The water was in short supply and only twice was Omne offered any and then just enough to wet his throat. His eyes were red from the dust; they burned from the sweat that ran down his face. His throat was so dry it was hard to swallow and it hurt to talk. His legs were so tired he could hardly drag them along. His head ached from the hours in the hot sun with no hat.

At last, when he thought he could go no farther, they stopped for the night. They set up camp near some cliffs and brought more of the hard bread and dried meat out of the packs and ate the simple meal. Sitting on the stony ground, Omne was almost too tired to eat. He would rather just lay on the ground and sleep but he knew he had to eat to gain his strength back. Though the men had pushed him on, they had not mistreated him. He wondered if maybe they thought he would be worth more if he had no bruises showing. One of the two men who he was afraid of did not come this time. He felt safer now. The other one was still hard on him, but he thought he would be safe as long as there was only one. Surely, he thought, the other man would protect him. He had not been chained since the day he had first arrived in the home camp.

Now as the men settled down for the night he was surprised when he was again chained to a small tree. But this time only one leg was put in chains and he had enough slack so he could stand up. He was given one skin to lay on and one more to cover with.

Long after the others had fallen to sleep Omne lay awake, thinking. He thought about the past six months. "It has been so long since I was taken away. How are my parents, brothers and sisters? Are they safe? Are they still looking for me? Will I ever see them again?" Then he thought of Amil. "I sure miss you my friend." The two young men had grown to love each other like brothers, depending on each other's friendship to endure the hard times. They worked together and consoled each other. What would become of Amil? "I wish he was here now."

Omne stared out over the barren, desolate land as the night deepened around him. Looking up into the darkening sky he whispered, "Is there a God up there? Do You really care about me or is the god in my home angry at me and punishing me for not liking him? Where are they taking me? What will happen to me?" A few tears started trickling down his dirty face in spite of his resolve to be strong. His life seemed empty. He could see nothing to place his hope on in his future. "Oh father, mother, I miss you!" Then a flood of tears burst like a broken dam, nearly washing his face clean from the dust of the trail. Finally he turned his gaze upward again and saw the stars. They were still bright, the same ones he had long ago learned to identify. Looking up he thought of what Amil had said just that morning.

"My God will help you. Pray to Him any time you want.; He is always near and is a God of love."

Now, even though Omne did not fully understand Amil's strange God, he again whispered quietly, "If there is a God up in the sky, I need You now. Will You help me as Amil said You would? If You are a God of love please let me see some of that love. I can't bare much more; I need help right now." Slowly his body began to relax as he whispered his prayer and at last he fell into a deep sleep.

About mid-day, on the third day, they entered a town. It was larger than Omne had ever seen but the men called it small. He was taken to a house on the edge of the town and placed in a locked room. This house was made of sun-dried clay and had a thatched roof. It was cool inside and Omne was thankful to be out of the hot sun. He was so tired and filthy, covered with sweat and dirt. Exhausted, he sank to the hard floor and started to sob. It was just too much for him to bare. His young body and soul were about broken.

At last his tears were spent and he began to think more rationally and to look around him. Again he remembered Amil. "My God is all powerful" Amil had told him. "My God will help you." Amil had also promised to pray to his God for him.

Now as he sat on the hard ground of the hut Omne thought of his prayer two nights ago. "Did Amil's God help me that night? I slept so well and did not grow weary all the next day. Last night I just fell asleep and did not pray; today I am tired and discouraged. Could it be?" he wondered.

"God," he began, "I don't know You. Are You there? Can You hear me? Amil said You would care for me. Well God, if You can, please help me. I don't want to be a slave. But if I have to be a slave, please let a kind man buy me. I am so weary. God, if You are there can You send someone to help me?" He thought of what he had just said as he walked around the small, dismal room. "I sure do need help now."

The room was so dirty with trash and filth covering the floor. It was bare except for a filthy mat on the floor in one corner and a table which was covered with filth. "Clearly," he thought, "someone, maybe many people, have been locked in this room for long periods of time; look at all that vomit and human waste on the floor.

Will that be my fate too?" he worried outloud. "It sure stinks in here and I am beginning to feel sick from the stench of it. But there is no way out, not even a small window to get fresh air through. I wonder how long I will be in here. Worse yet what will become of me?" He fought back the tears that again threatened to spill out of his sore eyes.

"I just can't let them know that I have cried. They will only make it harder for me," and he angrily wiped at the telling streaks.

The time drug slowly by and after several hours he knew why there was human waste on the floor. A person could only wait so long before relief. How long he was in the room he did not know but he knew it grew dark outside and he must have slept a little.

He was awaken by a loud commotion at the door and the door was swung open. Come with me the man at the door said. We are taking you to another place not far from here. A man there might buy you. If he doesn't we will have to take you to another place many miles away."

Omne realized that this was the man he feared the most and hung back out of the man's reach.

"Say, you are good looking. Maybe I should buy you." Fear shot through Omne as the man grabbed him and began pushing him back into the dark room. Struggling to get free Omne accidentally stepped on the man's foot.

"Hey, stop that," the man growled. "You are in my care now and will do as I say." He pushed Omne down on the mat, the young man falling hard. Then the man stood over Omne with an evil look showing in his eyes. "Take that," the man said as he gave Omne a hard kick to his thigh as Omne struggled to get up. "Now you do as I tell you or I will give you a beating you will never forget."

Just then a voice called out. "Hey, hurry up will you. Get that boy out here."

With a growl the man jerked Omne up on his feet. Then as he pushed the young man towards the door he snarled, "If you aren't sold, I will see you later," and he shoved Omne out the door. Omne had to catch himself as he was flung out the door. He flailed his arms in an effort to stop his fall. Steadying himself he looked up at the other man.

"Are you in a hurry," the other man asked as Omne gained his footing. "I guess that room is not the cleanest room."

"I just stumbled," Omne mumbled.

"Well we had better be on our way" and the man turned and headed towards the road followed by Omne and the other man. Omne tried to walk without a limp but his Left thigh was painful and hurt with every step. With sheer determination Omne hurried along.

The three walked for about an hour and stopped at a large ranch. Omne, by now, was more at ease and thankful to be out of the filthy room. Though still sore, his left thigh was not as painful as earlier. Even though the one man kept glaring at him Omne knew he was safe, at least for now. The two men put Omne in another locked shed and went away.

Omne looked around this new room. It was small but clean. There was a clean sleeping mat, one stool and a table. It had a fresh smell to it and with relief Omne sat on the stool to think. "Now God, are You still here? Was it You who saved me from that cruel man back there? If You are up there please send me help. Keep me from the evil ones. I am truly afraid of that man and don't want to see him any more." Again he had to fight back the tears.

It was but a short time before he heard a soft knock at the door and heard the latch open. He stiffened as the door opened, fearing it was that cruel man, then relaxed as he saw the one who entered.

There stood a young lady. She smiled at Omne and set a pail of hot water on the floor beside him. Handing him some soft cloths she said, "Here, wash up with this warm water. It will make you feel better. I will bring you some clean clothes to put on after you are cleaned. I don't understand why these men brought you here looking like you do. Still," and she paused to show her concern for him, "I know it was not your fault," and with that she was gone.

For a moment Omne just sat there. It was like a dream. Could it be real? He tested the water and it was warm. In wonder, he undressed and washed himself well with the warm water and soft cloths. On his left thigh he saw a large bruise, now dark and swollen. "At least," he thought, "there is no cut and it should heal soon." He was just finishing when he heard the knock on the door. In near panic lest she should see him he searched for something to cover himself with.

All he could find was his old dirty clothes. Hurriedly he covered his body and waited for the door to open. Again the young lady entered. This time she carried clean clothes for him to put on. Setting them on a stool, she left the room.

He was amazed at how much better the bath had made him feel and dressed in the clean clothes he felt like a new person. "Is God really looking after me?"

Again there was that soft knock on the door. This time she carried in a pot of delicious smelling stew. It was steaming and the aroma soon filled the whole room. "Here," she said. "Eat this. I will return later to get the pot." Then she added with a faint smile, "you do look better now. I hope you feel better too."

"OH, I do feel better but wait, can't you stay just a minute? Who are you? Did you buy me? What will happen to me?"

"I can not stay now. I will come later and maybe we can talk then. Right now I must go. If I stay in here too long the others will come looking for me. It will not be good."

"But I need to talk to someone. Please?"

"Later." And picking up his filthy rags she was gone.

The stew was as good as it smelled. It was the best food he had eaten since he had been taken from his home. He was so hungry that he ate all of it. He sat on the stool for what seemed to him like a long time. "She is not coming back. I knew it was too good to be true."

Then there was that soft knock on the door and she was there.

She left the door open as she sat on a stool near him. As he glanced towards the open door she said, "Don't go out. There are several men watching."

"Are they the ones who brought me here?"

"Yes," two of them are, and here she lowered her voice to barely a whisper. I don't understand how they can be so dirty. It must have been hard on you," and she let her smile linger just a moment on him. "They did not want me to bring you water to wash in or clean clothes. It seems to me that a clean, nicely dressed slave would sell for more then a filthy slave in dirty, smelly rags. They are evil men. They steal young boys and girls and sell them for slaves. They know that my master has a soft heart for strong young slaves so they bring them here. My master buys some but I do not think he will buy any more." Here she paused for a moment before adding, "you will be harmed if you try to get away. They did not want me to return. I finally convinced them to let me return if I left the door open. They look so cruel. I would hate to belong to them."

For a minute they just looked at each other. Then he spoke, "What is your name? Who are you?"

"I am Martha. I am also a slave here but I am treated like a family member. These folk are good to me. My own family all died and I had no where to go. These kind folk brought me here and cared for me. Now I work for them. They are good to me."

"Did they buy me?"

"No, you are here just for a few days. Then you will go. I don't know where you will go. Now I must go out. I will come later and I will also see if I can take you outside for awhile."

"Just a minute. If the ones who own you are so kind, would they buy me? I mean, I would rather go home to my own family, but if I can't go home I would like to be with kind people? You know what I mean?"

"Yes. I will see."

"I am also afraid of those men who brought me here; one of them threatened me just this morning. He would have harmed me if the other had not intervened. I am afraid he will come in here after you leave me."

"You will not be harmed as long as you stay in this room. Old Simeon is also out here and he will see that no harm comes to you. He knows the evil these men do and will watch." Again she was gone and he was alone. Again the loneliness filled him and he felt tears in his eyes. "LORD," he whispered as he wiped at his eyes, "if You love me like Amil said You do, please send me to a nice home."

CHAPTER 4

Martha returned when the sun was swinging to the western horizon and his stomach was telling him it was again empty. She brought him another bowl of stew plus some warm bread with some goat cheese. "Oh thank you," he said. "I am hungry. But I have been in here a long time and need out for a few minutes, even before I can eat."

"We already thought of this. Simeon is waiting outside and he will assist you."

"Come with me Omne. You will be safe as long as you do not try to get away," Simeon said to him.

Gratefully Omne followed Simeon. "Are the men who brought me here still around?"

"They left to go into the town for the night. We have no place here for the likes of them to sleep. I imagine they will also need more drink."

Later as he devoured his meal Omne thought about the people with whom he was now staying. The yard was not cluttered but neat and clean. There were no swine either. So far everyone he had met were polite to him. "I must ask Martha," he mused.

When Martha came to take the empty dishes away she said, "I will come soon and take you for a walk. Do not try anything as you will be watched."

Omne was glad to get outside again.

As they walked about the place Omne again spoke about him staying there.

"I spoke to the mistress about you. She said that she would talk to the master and see what might be done. What experience have you had? What work have you done?"

"Before I was taken I worked hard every day in the field. On my 14th birthday my father bought me my own team of oxen and I worked them most every day. I am used to doing hard work, especially if treated well." Hope sprang into his heart as he talked. "What god do you worship here?" he asked.

Startled, she said, "Why do you ask?"

"Well at my home we had a god who sat in the corner of the room. He was made of silver and mother said he was the strongest god. A friend of mine said his God was stronger. He could not see his God. Later when I was taken away there was another young man my age with whom I became good friends with. He talked about his God. It was the same God that my young friend earlier had worshipped. I asked him why he was also a slave. I did not understand why he was a slave if his God was so strong. He did not have enough time to tell me why, but he did say that his God would help me if I wanted him to."

"What does his God look like? Could you see him?"

"I don't know what his God looked like as I could not see him. Amil said his God lived in heaven but was also everywhere. He said his God ruled everything and everyone!"

"Ah! That is the same God we worship here. He is the Almighty God. He is the one who made all things. That is also why my people treat their slaves well."

"You are a slave too? Do they really treat all their slaves this well?"

"Yes. I have been here since I was a small girl. And yes, they treat all their slaves well. As long as the slave tries to cooperate he will be well treated."

"Do you think I will be able to stay here?"

"I do not know."

25

The next morning Omne was greeted by the master himself. "How old are you?"

"I am almost 16 years old."

"Tell me about your family. Why are you here?"

"My family live along ways from here. We had a small farm and raised wheat, grapes and sheep. I have 3 younger brothers and 3 younger sisters. I was taken by 5 rough men as I was plowing in the field."

"Did not your family try to help you?"

"I was alone at the time. I could not fight all the men and there was no place where I could escape to. So I did what they asked and they chained me to two of the men and took me to a far away land. I was there many months until they brought me here."

"I see. I was amazed and saddened to see you when the men brought you here.

You looked so tired, so filthy that I wondered how the men thought I would buy you. I wish there was a way to stop this slavery, especially when the likes of these men are involved. They are evil. But now I see you differently. I am thinking of buying you. I understand that you want to stay here. Is that right?"

"Yes. I can tell that you treat all your slaves well."

"Okay then. You will stay here. The work is hard, the hours are long. Are you man enough for it?"

"Yes."

"Very well then, you are now free. No not free to leave, but free to move about here at will. You will be closely watched until you prove yourself. You will be expected to work hard."

"I am not afraid of hard work. Really I feel better when I can do hard work. I also trust that you will treat me fairly if I do my best. Sir," and he paused to think, "Please sir, where are we? I mean what town is that town near here."

"The town is called Colosse."

"Colosse? I have heard of that city. Travelers going by my home talked about Colosse. I understand it is about 3 to 4 days travel from here to my home. Why did it take us so long to get here? We traveled for 3 days to get to where I stayed for awhile and another nearly 3 days to get here. I wonder why?"

"I am sure they took you to a remote area for fear they would be followed. Those who steal slaves do that.

They will steal and take the captives far away until they are sure they aren't being followed. They will then take them to another spot to sell them." Then looking closely at Omne the master continued, "were you thinking of running away all ready?"

"No sir. I do still miss home. But from what I see of the others here, I will be treated well here. I will serve you and do my best to please you. Besides I have no idea where my home is."

"If you do right you will be treated well. Now I have other matters to attend to. Simeon will come and help you get started with the work."

Omne worked hard. He was put in charge of a team of oxen and worked the fields from sun up until sunset. His master had several fields of grain along with a large vineyard. In one pasture there was a large flock of sheep. Omne had a few short breaks during these hours and soon grew familiar with the other workers. Often he would see Martha as she went about her work. She would sometimes bring him a cool drink as he worked. They said little but their eyes spoke what their mouths could not utter. She was most lovely to look upon and so thoughtful of all. He had already learned that she was just 7 months younger than he. Omne noted several other men who also watched her but she paid them little attention.

One day, after Omne had been here for nearly two years, the master's young son, a lad of 6 years old, was playing on the bank of the Lycus River which ran through the fields. He had been warned to stay away from the river as it was in flood stage. Now the river was a raging torrent, muddy and boiling in its madness. Like a demon it clawed and chewed away at the banks, tossing trees and other debris around as if they were small twigs. Seth was a good boy but had grown careless as he played. Never intending to get close to the river's edge, he was surprised when he saw the raging river so near. For a while he stood a short distance away from the bank, then he moved still closer to get a better look at the foaming water. "I have never seen the water so high or so muddy," he thought. "I have been here many times before with my friends, playing in the water but then the water was always clear and shallow, gurgling laughingly as it meandered through the valley. Also, even then, there was always an adult with us.'

Today as he stood there alone he felt more grown-up. Maybe this is why he crept even closer to the edge. Suddenly he felt the ground slipping away from under his feet. He had only enough time to utter one loud scream before he was in the water. He was rolled over and over by the strong current. As his head surfaced he again screamed. Gasping for air, he again was rolled over and sank into the raging water. Light was fading and he was going down again.

On this day Omne was plowing with his team of oxen in the field, enjoying at last a sunny day. It had rained so much for days. Even now the land was wet, a little too wet to plow, but he dared not wait longer. As he walked slowly behind the team he looked at the dark, wet soil as it was turned over. It was slow work but by keeping at it he would finish this field by night. His body had filled out with age and hard work. His dark eyes had a light in them and his black hair lay wind blown. He had an assurance about him that caused respect from others.

Then he thought of Martha and even here alone in the field he could feel warmth come to his face.

The very thought of her quickened his pulse and sent shivers of delight throughout his whole being. Then checking himself he said outloud, "I can't expect to ever have her. I am just a slave with no rights. I must somehow forget this silly dream."

He was just turning the team to go back when he heard a scream. Instantly he stopped the team and strained to listen. He was not far now from the river's edge and could hear the roar of the water. Hearing nothing but the water he was about to start his work again when he heard another scream. Running quickly to the water's edge he looked over the raging water. Finally downstream he thought he could see a small form sinking in the water.

He rushed on towards the form and just as it sank he saw it was a child. Without thinking for his own life he jumped into the water. His breath was knocked out of him as he hit the cold water. He sank into its muddy realm. Hitting the bottom he pushed himself up for air. As his head popped out of the water he took in a large gulp of air. At the same time he saw the child just a little distance from him, sinking again. Diving again he grabbed the boy's clothes and fought to make it to the shore. Struggling against the current he pushed his way through the murky water. His legs and arms grew tired and it was difficult to keep his head above the water. Many times he would open his mouth to take in a deep breath only to have it filled with muddy water instead. He was just about to give up when his feet touched bottom and he found he could stand up in the water. Mustering all his strength he hoisted the boy out of the water, and climbed out. As tired as he was he could not rest yet. He rolled the boy over and pounded on his back. Water gushed out of the boy's mouth and Omne was relieved to hear the boy gasp for air. As the boy's breathing grew stronger and the color returned to his skin, Omne gasped, "Seth," he whispered, "what are you doing here?" Then without waiting for an answer he picked him up in his strong arms and carried him to his master's house.

Omne reached the house only to fall at the doorway, his strength used up and his body unable to move any farther.

He lay crumpled like a pile of rags at the very threshold of safety but knew it not.

Omne never knew when he was helped to his mat. He didn't see the fear in Martha's eyes as she called for help. He did not feel the strong arms lift him up and carry him, placing him gently on his own mat. Later, like a dream he heard voices all around but could not answer them. He struggled to respond to their commands but had no power to do so. Then he felt warmth flooding over his body. It was a wonderful feeling and as his body began to warm up he tried to move and finally opened his eyes. For a moment he could not move as he was held tightly in place. Fear shot through him as he struggled to free himself. Remembrance of the raging water tore through his mind as he fought to get free.

"Okay, Omne! Lie still. Do not fight us, you are safe, just relax! It is fine now!"

Slowly his body relaxed and he became more aware of his surroundings. Turning his head he realized that he was tightly squeezed between two men. When he had tried to move the ones lying tightly on both sides of him slowly moved away. Turning his head to the right he looked into his master's eyes. Shock flooded across his face and he looked quickly away only to find Old Simeon lying close on his left." Terror filled his eyes as he remembered that evil man of years ago.

"Do you not remember what happened? About you risking your life to save Seth. You carried him to our doorstep and there you collapsed. I am not sure how long you laid there for when Seth came in all wet, both his mother and I worked over him to dry and warm him. It was only after he was warmer that he was able to tell us what had happened to him.

It was Martha who found you crumpled at our door.

"Omne," Seth had cried. "Where is Omne? He carried me to the door and fell there. You have to help him."

You were very cold when we found you and we carried you to your mat. We covered you with covers but you did not respond to anything we did. We needed to get you warmed and knew of only one way. That is why we were lying tightly next to you."

"Yes," added Simeon. You were like ice and about froze me. Burr were you cold. If you had not warmed soon I would have had to have someone warm me," and here the older man chuckled outloud.

Omne lay still as he struggled to remember. "Oh now I remember. Seth?" and a new fear filled his eyes. "Is he okay? I tried to save him. I think of him like he was my little brother. Where is he?" Tears stood out on his eyelashes as he looked from one to another.

"Seth is fine. Call him in so Omne can see him." The master was now smiling at him. "You did a wonderful thing. How can I ever thank you enough?"

Seth entered the room and stood by Omne's sleeping mat. He looked at Omne with bright, moist eyes. Are you okay Omne?"

"I am fine. What I don't understand is how I saved you. I had never been in water before except for a bath. I never learned to swim. Yet I remember that rushing, muddy water and seeing you in it I never even thought. I just knew that I had to save you and so I jumped in."

Turning to look at his master he continued, "did I really save him? I must have had help. Who helped me?"

"You did it alone. But I am sure our God helped you. He is all Mighty and loves us."

"Your God helped me? Why? I don't even know him."

"He knows your heart. And we know him. Now I want you to rest a little longer. We will talk later. But first drink this hot drink for it will help warm you."

After he was alone, Omne pondered what had happened and how it had come to pass. He was thinking about this God, the God who loves people, when he fell into a sweet sleep.

It was late in the day when Omne again awoke. When he saw the position of the sun in the sky he leaped out of his bed in haste. He had work to do. His master would be angry with him. Hurriedly he put his clothes on and walked into the sunlight on his way to get his team but was stopped by Martha.

She was bringing him some food. It looked and smelled so good that he immediately realized how hungry he was. She did not have to tell him. He went to his eating place and sat down. He ate his fill and felt new strength flow through his body.

He had just finished his meal when the master came. Jumping to his feet, Omne started to apologize. "I am sorry sir! I should have been in the field long ago. I will get right at it," and he looked worriedly at his master.

"Hold on there fellow. You can get back to it tomorrow.

"tomorrow? I have to take care of the oxen."

They are already in their stalls. Now I want to talk to you. What can I do to show you how much I appreciate your saving Seth."

"Why sir, I only did what anybody would have done. My reward was just seeing that boy alive and smiling at me. I need no reward. You are good to me. And I love that little boy too."

"That is fine Omne. But I think I know of what I can do for you. Do you like Martha?"

"Martha? Why sure I do. She is a beam of sunshine whenever she is near me. Why do you ask?" Here Omne felt again that warm sensation he felt every time he looked at Martha. Trying to stifle these thoughts he looked at his master and listened with wonder at what he heard.

32

"Would you like her for your wife?"

"My wife? But why? I am still here hardly two years. There are others who have been here longer and I know more than one of them who would like her."

"That is all true. But you are one of the best workers here and I feel you would treat her well. As for the others, Daniel, and Othnieal who you refer to, well I will never let one of them have Martha. Never! he said again. Now what do you say? Would you like Martha for your wife?"

Even without Omne saying a word the master could tell the answer. There was a light in Omne's eyes, a sparkle that danced merrily as the young man contemplated this news.

"Oh sir, I say yes. How did you know that this was the dream of my life. To marry Martha is the best joy I could ever know. But shouldn't we ask Martha? Maybe she will not want me."

"I tell you what. You ask her tonight when she comes in with your food. I know what she will say."

"Okay," was all he could answer.

Martha seem flustered when she brought him his food. She used to bring it to him but after he was trusted, he was free to go as he pleased and he ate with the others.

"You look pretty, Martha. Will you sit with me while I eat? Are you hungry too?"

"I will sit here but I am not hungry."

"Martha, I am sure you already know what I am going to say. I don't know how to say it. Here goes. Martha, will you be my wife? I think I have loved you from the first time I saw you. But I figured that for me it was impossible to marry you so I have tried to not think of this. Now I know I can if you will agree. Will you be my wife?" and he searched her face for the answer, fearful that even yet she would refuse him this great joy.

"Yes I will. I am so glad it is you. I too love you."

He reached for her hand and pulled her to him. "You are more than I even hoped for. I love you."

CHAPTER 5

The wedding was a simple affair. Had they been true children of the family it would have been an elaborate affair, but as they were both slaves, even well loved slaves, it was most simple. The couple was given a small cottage of their own to live in but their duties remained the same. Both had to work as hard as before and this began the day after their wedding. Yet this was not a problem for both were used to hard work. Just being together made their hard toil worthwhile.

Though they seldom saw the other during the busy day, Martha would at times carry a cool drink to Omne. These encounters, though brief, brought joy to each.

Their love for each other made their work easier and they worked harder at their tasks. Both the master and his wife were well pleased with the outcome.

In the evenings after their work was done, Omne and Martha would often walk along the stream that ran through the fields. Then, while sitting on a large rock under an old gnarled tree, they would talk quietly together. Here they were secluded from all others and would hold each other close as they relaxed from their hard day's work. Other times they would stroll, along the river while they surveyed the ever-changing landscape. Looking

North they could see the distant buildings that stood on the edge of Colosse.

All around them were low mountains and hills. Situated in a valley, Colosse and the neighboring villages and farms were hemmed in by the low hills. The valley floor was a fertile land. Grain and grapes were raised there. Herds of sheep and goats roamed the hills and smaller valleys. The land was mostly open, with but a few scrubby trees and some thorny bushes. Some rain would fall nearly every month, thus the grain grew well. In places there were also a few olive groves. In the sub-tropic weather it was seldom very cold, though it did get cool at night, especially in the mountains. There might be a few times in the winter months when even in the valleys it would get quite cool but these times were rare. All in all it was a lovely land. Omne and Martha felt safe and content here.

One night as they lay on their sleeping mat, Martha asked Omne about his family.

"I have 3 brothers and 3 sisters, all younger than I am. My parents are kind." At this his voice drifted away as his eyes took on a distant stare. For a moment the hurt of his separation from his family nearly overwhelmed him and he wiped his eyes quickly to hide his feelings.

"You still miss them a lot don't you?"

"Yes at times it is most difficult for me. I am sure that they are also hurting over my disappearance. Now my next brother will have to do more work. We were very close and used to do everything together. But he was not as strong as I and he did not have to work as hard either. Now it will be worse on him." Well enough of this. I can't do anything about it now. It won't help to fret over it." Then taking Martha in his arms he added, "I am so thankful that I have you as my wife. I can never tell you how much you mean to me or how much you have helped me. I love you so much,"

"I feel the fortunate one," whispered Martha. You are all I desire." Her eyes were moist with her happiness.

But not all here in this peaceful land were pleased with the turn of events. Daniel and Othnial were not happy at all. Especially Daniel. He had long sought the affection of Martha and was much indignant that she was given to Omne. He went around with the look of a wounded animal, always defensive and argumentative. He often told Othnial, "I will get even with Omne, just you wait and see. He will be sorry he ever married Martha."

With a sneer Othnial would reply, "Do you think Omne had a choice? When one is a slave he does what he is told to do. I too don't like Omne but I can't do anything about it now." In his heart Othnial was upset that Martha had not been given to him for he too had yearned for her. He did not love her but wanted her to use as he pleased. So he too carried a grudge against Omne and searched for a way to get his revenge.

One day Daniel's chance came. He had found a large thorn bush the day before as he worked near the edge of his field and he gathered some of the large thorns.

"Look what I have," Daniel said to Othnial that evening.

"So! What is so great about thorns? What good are they?" Othnial looked with scorn at his friend.

"You will see what good they are," sneered Daniel. "You just watch what I do with them tomorrow!"

The next day as Omne was taking a short rest, Daniel went quickly to Omne's team. Placing the large thorns under the harness straps he made sure that the harnesses were not pulled tight, then slipped away before Omne returned.

When Omne returned and commanded the team to go forward, the thorns dug into their skin as the harnesses tightened. This sharp pain in their sides made the oxen jump and move faster. Omne had great difficulty in controlling them. They had gone over 50 feet before Omne could stop them. They were still trembling as he walked up to them.

"What is the matter with you? You know better than to act like this." As he talked to them he noted something sticking out from under one of the harness straps. Gently he raised the strap and there was a large thorn. He stood in shock as he surveyed the thorn. Gently, very gently he eased the thorn out. Carefully he searched over the animals and removed a dozen more thorns. Several had punctured the skin and small drops of blood formed on the oxen's sides. These spots would need treatment to avoid infection.

Making sure the team was again calm, he instructed them to remain still while he hurried to the barn to get the medicine.

Returning to his team he spotted Daniel hurrying away from the team. "I wonder what he was doing over here," Omne said to himself. "He is supposed to be working in that field over on the other side of the river." He walked quickly up to his team. Speaking softly to them he started to apply the medicine. The great beasts were still trembling slightly as they let him apply the soothing medicine.

"Now I know why Daniel was here!" There are new thorns under the oxen's harnesses. "Why would he do this? What have I done to him?"

Again Omne carefully removed them and put the medicine on the wounds. He pondered as to just what he should do about this matter.

While he was walking back to the plow, he spotted thorns and thorn seeds scattered over a large area of the freshly plowed ground. If left there, these seeds would sprout and grow thorns with the grain. Patiently he tried to pick up all the seeds. "Why would Daniel do this?" he wondered. It took several minutes to gather the thorn seeds but finally Omne was satisfied that he had done his best. Now he could only hope that he had not missed even one thorn seed but fear shot through him as he knew there were probably many seeds that he had not found.

That evening the master happened out into the field that Omne was working in. "Say Omne, what happened over there?

Did you have a problem? It also looks like you did less work today. Why?"

Omne did not know what to say. He hesitated for a moment before he answered. "Sir, the oxen acted up some. I had trouble getting them to settle down."

"Are you losing control over them?"

"No sir. I don't think so."

"Well better be more careful. I would hate to think that you are getting sloppy now. Maybe marriage is not the best for you after all." Then before Omne could reply, the master walked away never once looking back at the stricken young man who was now standing with downcast face and gloom filling his whole being.

Onne was very quiet that night as he went home. Martha tried to find out what was wrong but he wouldn't tell her.

"Do you not love me like you used to? Did I do something wrong?" Tears started down her lovely face as she looked at Omne. Her body shook with shivers of fright as she waited for his reply. "Oh what did I do?"

"Oh Martha! You did not do anything wrong." Going to her he wrapped his arms around her and pulled her to him. "I love you more than ever before. You are the most important one in my life."

"Then please tell me what is bothering you."

"I am sorry dear. I do not want to worry you. But I see I will have to tell you. Today Daniel tried to get me in trouble." The words tumbled out as a raging stream boils in its haste to reach the valley below. He ended with saying, "Now I don't know what I should do. Even the master thinks I am not doing my best."

"The master knows better than that. Shouldn't you tell him?"

"If he thought I was doing my best why did he get after me so angrily today? What could I say to his outrage? That spot in the field does not look nice; it is not as smooth as the rest of the field. So how can I go to the master?"

"The master would listen to you. I am sure he would believe you. I know he is well pleased with you. You must talk to him."

"How can I? Daniel has been here a long time, much longer then I. Will not the master think I am just trying to get Daniel in trouble?"

"Well I don't know why Daniel did this but I will pray he leaves you alone."

"Bless the God for giving you to me," he replied."

While they talked into the night Omne said, say, when I first came here the master used to slay a lamb and place it on the alter.

I understand it was as a sacrifice to your God. But now he doesn't offer sacrifices anymore. Do you know why? Is he not afraid of offending his God?"

I too have wondered over this matter. I asked the mistress once but we were too busy for her to tell me all. But she will tell me tomorrow if she has the time. I will tell you. I never did like to see animals sacrificed. The sacrifice of the animals pointed forward to the future coming of our God to this earth."

"Your God is to come to our Earth? When?"

"Soon. Now we had better get to sleep if we are to get up in time in the morning. Good night my love."

"Good night."

The next day went well for Omne. He whistled as he worked and the master coming by, unnoticed by Omne, smiled to himself. "Here is a good worker. In fact he is my best worker."

Martha too had a good day. The mistress had her come into her private room and there she shared with her the news. She said, "our God came several years ago but the wicked people killed him. Still when one reads all the prophecies of God's coming, it pointed out that this was just the way it would be. He was killed that others might have life. But he is not dead," she added.

"Not dead!" Martha said in confusion, "But you said that evil men killed him?"

"Yes, that is true! But you see, he rose on the third day as it had been written about in prophecy years ago. Now he has ascended to heaven and is there helping to save his people. As the sacrifice of lambs and oxen pointed forward to his coming, it is no longer necessary to offer sacrifices. This God was our sacrifice for all times for all who would believe. One day this God will return and take his people home to heaven with him. There in heaven all will be the same; there will be no slaves or owners of slaves. All will be free," her mistress said.

This new teaching was not easy for Omne and Martha to believe. Many days they studied with the master and mistress and day by day the joy of this new teaching replaced the fear of the old way. Their God was alive, He loved them so much that he gave his life for them. He was coming again for them. Glory to God.

With this new teaching the master and mistress were even better to their slaves. All were given longer rest periods, more time off. As the slaves better understood the new teaching, their work also improved. Thus they did more work in less time.

Another reason that Martha was happy that day was that she was soon to give Omne a child. She was so excited as she told Omne the news.

The spring had given the needed rain and now as the summer's heat fell on the land the grain grew well; its green shoots covering the dark dirt of yesterday.

Omne's field of grain grew evenly and promised to give a bountiful harvest. That is all but one area; this one was full of thorns and the grain had to struggle to grow. With mounting frustration Omne surveyed the spot. He had not found all the seeds! Now he couldn't pull them out or he would pull out the grain too. He would have to wait until the harvest. Omne knew he had to tell the master and though this thought struck him with fear he knew it had to be done. "Well I might as well do it now and get it over with," he said to himself. "The master will be angry with me," and Omne's shoulders drooped as he thought of his master's angry words a few months ago.

The master smiled at Omne as he opened the door to his knock. But his smile faded as he looked at his faithful slave for clearly something was wrong.

"Omne, what is the matter? What has happened? Are you ill? Is it Martha?"

"We are fine."

"Then tell me what is wrong. Do not hide it from me as I can tell that you are in great distress."

"Sir, I didn't do a good job last spring on that lower field for now there is a patch of thorns growing there. If I had done my job well there would not be thorns there. It looks very bad!" He hung his head in disgrace as he waited for his master to reply.

"I see. Shall we go have a look at them?"

Arriving in the field near the thorns the master surveyed the scene before him. "Yes, there are many thorns. There has been no thorns here for years. I wonder how the seeds got here. Do you have an answer? Did you scatter thorn seeds here?" He studied the young man as he spoke.

"No sir, I did not plant thorn seed but I planted only the good grain you gave me to plant!" His eyes were moist with fear as he stood there midst the ugly thorns.

"Isn't this the same spot where you had trouble with the team last spring?"

"Yes it is," Omne answered quietly.

"Want to tell me about it?"

"Sir, I don't want to."

"Do you not know that neither Daniel or Othnial are here anymore?"

Omne jerked his head up and stared with fear into his master's eyes. He searched for anger but saw only kindness. Lowering his head he started to reply, "I didn't.

But the master cut him off. "Do you want to know why. I will tell you. I had been watching them for a long time. Frequently problems would arise and one or both of them were always involved. I also knew of your distrust of them, especially after I had given Martha to you.

"You knew?" Omne whispered. "But I never told anyone!"

"Yes, I knew! I started keeping even closer track of them. Old Simeon was also a spy for me. It was Simeon who had seen what Daniel did to your team that day. He also knew about the thorn seed, knew that Othnial had scattered the seed. The next day Martha came to work and showed that something was bothering her. When my wife pressed her for the reason she told her what had happened. But you see, I already knew."

"You knew all the time. When you came to the field and harshly reprimanded me you already knew?"

"Yes I knew. But I knew something that you did not know. I knew that both Daniel and Othnial were watching from a hidden spot. I was testing them one more time. I also knew that you tried to pick up all the thorn seeds. You did all you could. You only did one thing wrong."

Fearfully Omne asked, "What did I do wrong?"

"You didn't tell me what had happened. Why?"

"I am sorry sir. I only knew that I was still new here and the other two had been here a long time. I have never been one to tell tales on another. I didn't want to make trouble for anyone."

"I understand. But in this you protected the wrong people. In these serious matters I need to be told."

"I am sorry. I was so afraid that if I told they would make more trouble for me. I will remember from now on."

"Fine. Now we had better get to work. Except for that one spot your fields look better than any of the others.

It shows your good work. Soon it will be harvest time. I will help you bind up the thorns before they go to seed."

"You, sir?" Omne asked in consternation. "Not you!"

"Why not me?" the master asked, a smile playing across his face. "Of course I will help you. I will enjoy doing this work when it is time." The master smiled at the young man who stood looking in amazement at him. "We should be able to harvest the grain first."

There was a good harvest that fall and the thorns were all bundled and burned before they could spread their seed over the soil.

The harvest was just in when Omne and Martha's baby came. He was a healthy boy, a joy to his parents. In fact the master and mistress acted like they were the grandparents. The mistress helped care for the baby, named Jared after Omne's father, while Martha worked in the house for her.

Over the next several years more babies came along. Soon there were seven little tots, all loved as the first. Their life was a good one, hardly resembling that of a slave. In fact Omne and his family were treated like the children of the master and mistress, whose only child, Seth, was now a young man.

Seth was a great help to all and remained a close friend to Omne. He never forgot how Omne had saved him from the raging river and treated Omne like an elder brother, not a slave. Often the two would work together.

Omne was now the head slave, taking Simeon's place when Simeon grew too old for work. Omne was a good foreman and was respected by all, slaves and owners.

There were often meetings in the large house, and all were invited. Sabbath services were also held here. In days past the master had forgotten some of his beliefs and his slaves had worked every day. But with the coming of his new faith, everyone had the Sabbath off. Work was ceased in mid-afternoon on the 6th day and not resumed until early on the first day of the week. Yet even with this day off, the slaves accomplished more in 6 days than they had before in 7 days.

Neighboring slave owners scoffed when they heard that the slaves here had a day off. There was a few, though, who asked the master why he gave his slaves a day off and were later convinced of the truth. These other slave owners, when they put these teachings into practice, also gained a blessing. But it was only a few who believed.

One day Jared became ill. At first his parents were not too worried. He would be better in a few days. But he only grew worse. The best doctors were called in and the teachers were called in. They anointed and prayed for Jared's recovery. Still as the days passed the boy grew worse.

One day Jared called his parents, along with his brothers and sisters, to him. "I know that I am going to die soon."

"No son, don't say that."

"Yes father, I will soon die. Now please don't mourn long for me after I am gone. You can be sure that I am ready and the next thing I will know is my God calling me home at the time of the end. I want to see all of you there. Promise me that you will remain true to God!" Looking at his younger brothers and sisters he asked, "Will you meet me there? There will be many temptations along the way. Please promise me that you will be faithful. Will you?"

"Yes," they all answered.

"Now please call the master, mistress and Seth to me."

When they entered he looked long at them. "I love you as if you were really my own family.

45

Please remember the faith and keep it always. I want to see you at the resurrection. I am so glad my family is with you. Please help each other."

With this talk over he closed his eyes and went to sleep. Everyone walked quietly so as not to awaken him. They were still sure that he would get well. But that night he fell asleep, the sleep of death.

His funeral was a large affair. There was much weeping even though they had faith for the future. The loss was so great.

Omne suffered the greatest. Somehow he just could not cope or accept his son's death. He grew moody and his work suffered.

Martha understood his loss as she too suffered, but she longed to be able to talk to Omne. Still he would not talk to her about their loss. "You know I lost him too," she said. "I also loved him much. You aren't the only one who is suffering."

"I know Martha. Yet I don't understand why your God let this happen."

"My God! Isn't he your God too?"

"How can he be my God when he killed my son?"

"First remember he was my son too. Secondly, he didn't kill Jared. That was the results of sin caused by the evil one."

"But he allowed it to happen. He could have stopped it. At least if he is all powerful as we thought, he could have."

"I will not lose my faith in my God. Please, Omne, let God help you. He loves you still."

"I can't."

Weeks went on and still Omne brooded. No one could reach him. His work suffered greatly and others had to do what he should have done. Many times the master would talk gently to him about this problem. "Omne, I know you are missing your son. I don't understand why he died but we will see him again. Don't you believe this? You are like a son to me and it grieves me to see you carry that heavy load. Let God have it before it kills you."

But Omne would only shake his head and go his
way. What could he say? His gloom deepened; his
despondency grew darker.

One day the master had another one do work that
Omne was supposed to do. This was a job that Omne
like doing, still he was not getting at it. When
he saw another slave doing it he was devastated.
But instead of reasoning out as to why another was
doing his work, Omne only became more distraught.
He finally made a decision. He would leave! There
was no one here worth staying for. He did not
remember Martha's undying love for him; or how much
her love meant to him. He forgot his other
children, the little ones he loved and cherished.
He forgot how well his master treated him. Most of
all he forgot his God.

Omne needed some extra money but he knew where
his master kept some. This he stole and when the
others awoke in the morning, he was gone.

CHAPTER 6

When Martha awoke Omne was gone. She had not heard him get up but this was not unusual; he would often get up early without waking her and feed his team of oxen before returning to the house for his morning meal. She dressed and started preparing their meal. The children would be up soon and want their food. Omne would also be ready and hungry. She busied herself and soon had the morning meal ready, but Omne did not come. Turning to the now oldest child, David, she said, "Run to the barn and tell your father we are ready to eat."

A few minutes later David burst into the house. "Mother, father is not in the barn. I asked another man there if he had seen father and he said he had not seen him. Father's oxen are still in their stalls. No one has seen him."

"Go to the master's house and see if he is there."

Before long David returned again bringing the master with him.

"Martha," spoke the master, I have not seen Omne this morning. But I discovered something else. I found the empty box that I keep my money in.

It was on the ground just outside the house door. Omne knew where I kept it. I don't think anyone else knew the hiding spot. It looks like he took it. Why I do not know. He has not been

acting well since Jared died. Do you have any idea
where he might have gone?"

"Oh," Martha whispered. "I don't think Omne
would steal. I know he has been very depressed but
he surely would not steal."

"Any idea who would?"

"No."

"Well it looks like he did. He will be here
soon I am sure. When he comes I know he will
answer all our questions. Maybe he went to town to
buy that new plow that we need. He knew I was
planning to get it today anyway!" Then looking
intently at Martha he continued, "I am sure he will
soon be here; don't worry," and with that the
master left the house.

Martha set food before her family but did not
sit down to eat. Instead she left the house.
Going to a secluded spot near the creek she poured
out her heart to her God. "God, where is Omne? Has
he left? God, you know how depressed he has been
since Jared died. I don't understand either why he
had to die, but I accept it as your will. Oh be
near to Omne. He has been a good man. You know
where he is and why he is there. If he is in
danger please protect him.

If he is running from this depression please
comfort him. My God, please guide him and bring
him back. Keep him from evil men. I need him. I
love him so. Now the master is upset with him. He
thinks Omne stole from him. Omne would never do
that. He is a good man." With that she buried her
face in her hands and sobbed out her frustration
and fears.

Finally her body relaxed and she prayed, "Help
me to continue on. Help me care for my children.
I don't want them to hate their father. Help me to
carry on with the work that I have to do. Give me
the strength to go on and please be with Omne.
Bring him home soon. Thy will be done."

Washing her face in the stream's cool water, she
stood up and slowly returned to the house. Her

children needed her and her mistress would be
waiting for her.

In the days and weeks that followed she never
spoke badly about Omne. She encouraged the
children to continue to pray for their father and
to remember their love for him. She tried to keep
a smile on her face and life went on. Yet when all
were asleep for the night her resolve to be brave
would weaken and she would weep into her pillow.

The master and mistress could not understand why
Omne had left. Though they were hurt they still
missed him. Their relationship with Martha and the
children remained the same as before and they found
little ways to help.

* *

On a lonely trail that wound into the wild
countryside walked a sorrowful man. His shoulders
drooped while fear and confusion etched deep
furrows across his tanned face. He walked as one
who had no hope, at times nearly falling under the
unseen weight he carried on his shoulders.

He had no idea where he was going. He just knew
he had to flee. "God," he muttered. "You are
called a God of love? Where is that love? I don't
want anything to do with you if your love is to
kill at random, even little ones. Get out of my
life and leave me alone!" Even in his stupor he
was shocked at his words. But his depression had
turned to anger and he had to lash out at someone.

He was heading North West and was climbing into
the mountains. It was not a hard climb but he felt
the strain of the morning. Hours past and daylight
arrived. With daylight came hunger pains, for in
his hurry to flee he had neglected to pack much
food. What he had with him would only last this
day.

All that day he pushed on stopping only to rest
a few minutes or to get a drink from the stream he
was following. He ate sparingly of the little food
he had with him and watched as this scant supply

diminished. He continued on like one possessed or being hunted. Every strange sound brought increased fear to his heart.

That night he found a sheltered spot among some small trees and tried to sleep. He shivered in the growing darkness and cool night's air. His heart was too full of fear to allow much sleep. When he did sleep he thought of Jared or Martha. He could see Martha's face with pleading in her eyes as she looked at him. Even in his dream she did not scold him but pleaded for him to come home. He would awake in a cold sweat and feel hot tears flooding down his face. "Oh," he moaned, "will this night never end?"

The morning sun was just coming over the Eastern horizon when Omne set off again. He was on a lonely trail and had no idea where he was or where he was going. He just knew he had to go on and leave all he had ever known far behind. His strength weakened as the second night drew on. His meager food was all gone now and he had seen no water from which he could drink for several hours. His whole body ached, his stomach hurt from hunger and his throat was sore from thirst as he lay near the trail for the night.

On the third day he again pushed on as soon as the sun was up. "How much longer can I go without food?" he wondered. "Is there no one living near here?" He thought of praying but then remembered he had ran away from the only God who could help him. He was on his own.

"Well," he thought, "if I don't get food and water soon I won't have to worry about life any more. Maybe that will be best! I don't want to live anyway! I can't live without Martha but I can't return home either!"

At one point the trail followed a deep ravine. Stopping to look down the steep gorge he thought of just jumping over the side. "That may end it all," he said to himself. But for some reason he could not do it. Maybe it was fear of pain, maybe it was that he really did want to live, but he turned away and continued his way.

He had been on the trail for about six hours that day when he rounded a bend in the road and spied a house. A man and a woman were out in front of the house and had a fire burning. Going over to them he asked, "Could I get a drink of water and maybe you could spare a little bread."

Looking at the stranger the man motioned to his wife to fix him a little food. Then turning to Omne he said, "Come with me and I will get you a drink of cool water."

Omne drank like one dying of thirst, feeling the refreshing coming to his throat and whole being. When at last he was satisfied he turned to the man. "Thank you," that was so good."

"Where are you from, stranger?" Are you going a long way?"

"I am from Colosse. I am going to Greece to see my father who is not well," he lied. "I have money to pay for my food.

I thought it would be better to travel light and buy food on the way."

"You came all the way from Colosse? No wonder you are so thirsty. You obviously do not know this trail. It will not be an easy route and there are few houses along the way. Good thing you stopped here. Why did you come this way if you were going to Greece? This is sure the long way to get there when you could have gone a much shorter route. We had better send some extra food along with you to keep you as you go. You may not find another place to get food until you are near the sea." The man shook his head in wonder at this stranger.

The man's wife soon had food ready and Omne ate his fill. It was simple food but then he was used to that. They chatted as he ate, the man obviously interested in Omne. Omne was still a good looking man and other than his worry lines, looked very young.

"Omne," he spoke at last. "I can tell you are worried. I hope your father will be fine. But you must be very careful. Many men will not treat you well. Traveling alone you will be subjected to robbers and the like. It is not a safe road. Do not for any reason travel on it after dark. After you cross the pass and drop down into the valley, you will cross a river. It should not be dangerous at this time. About 2 hours walk from there you will come to a small village. As you enter it you will cross a small stream.

Just across that stream you will come to a small house. Stop there. The man there will help you."

"Why are you helping me thus? You don't even know me."

"I can tell that you are a good man and very worried. Now you are tired. I think you had better spend the night here with us and allow your body to rest and revive. You look like you could use a good sleep.

"No my friend," Omne answered. "I have to be going as I am not sure how long my father might be alive."

"Do not push to hard or you will fall by the wayside. You will reach the small village on the third day. Before it gets dark tonight you must stop and set up camp for yourself. You will not cross the pass until tomorrow night. Tonight stop before you climb high or you will be too cold during the night. Then If you walk fast you will cross the pass tomorrow afternoon. About half way down the other side it will start to get warmer. Find a secluded spot there for the night. Do not go to the valley as it will not be safe for you there at night."

"Why are you so kind to me?"

"I am a Christian. We need to help those in need. This is what Jesus taught us, to love one another. We are to be kind to everyone."

"You are a good man. Thank you for the food and the instructions. I too used to believe like you but God was hard on me.

How can I love a God like that? But if you can, well that is fine. It is true that I am glad you are like you are. You might have robbed me for I did not know anything about you when I stopped here. Here is some money for your help."

"Keep your money. We did not do much for you. You will need the money more later. As for you stopping here, I think our God had you stop here. Whether you like him or not, he is still watching out for you. He still loves you."

"Well I don't know about that. I don't need his help. I can do it on my own. Especially with help from those like you. Thank you my friend. I had better be on my way," and Omne set off at a brisk walk for he had to get to his next rest area before dark. The man's voice kept ringing in his ears. "Danger. Be most careful."

All that afternoon he continued, pausing only for rest breaks and to eat of the food the strangers had sent with him. He found a secluded spot and stopped for the night just as the sun was setting.

After another restless night he started on his way. He was climbing higher now and the air was growing cooler. He was most thankful for the food and goat-skin flask the man had given him. Now he was able to carry water with him so he need not grow thirsty.

At last he crossed the pass and started down.

It had been cold on the top and he was glad for the hard walk as it helped to keep him warm. As he descended the other side he noticed that it did indeed get warmer. He began looking for a place to sleep for the night. There was no good hiding spot that he could find. All that grew there were small juniper trees and some small bushes. There were a lot of large rocks and stones. Searching carefully he finally found what he thought would be a good place to hide and sleep for the night. He hoped that no one could see him from the trail but as he lay on the hard ground he was worried. The man's words kept reminding him of danger!

He ate some of the food he still had and tried to get comfortable on the ground. It was so hard, the many stones poking him through his clothing. He wondered why he was so worried. Why he had not been that worried since he was first taken from his parents home many years ago. Then he had been just a boy. Now he was a man. Why should he be scared? He lay shivering in the growing cold, wishing it was already daylight.

Then he heard a twig snap on the trail below him. He froze in place, terror on his face. Listening, all was again silent and he began to relax. At long last he fell into a fitful sleep.

He saw Martha and the children.

They were smiling at him. He tried to go to them but was held back by an unseen force. He screamed for help and Martha and the children were gone and he awoke to find it was only a dream. Again he dreamed and saw Jared. The boy was looking at him with sorrow. "Why did you do it father?" And so the night slowly dragged on.

It was still dark when he awoke with a start. What had awaken him? He lay in terror as again the sound came. Then he heard muffled voices on the trail below. He could not hear what they were saying, but gathered that they knew he was there. What could he do now? Oh God, where are you. But he had prayed in fear and frustration and not as a plea. He thought of praying but remembered that he now had no god.

Suddenly they were upon him. Blows fell fast and furious as he lay on the ground. He was kicked in the body and on the head. He felt a large blow fall on him and blackness descended.

How long he lay there he did not know. But when he again opened his eyes he saw it was late in the day. He tried to move but pain shot through his whole being. He lay still for awhile. Again he tried to move and this time he slowly turned to a crouching position. Finally he stood, pain racking his whole body. He was relieved to find that he had no broken bones, but every sinew of his body hurt. His head throbbed. He knew that he had to get out of here and do it quick. They might be back and this time they might kill him.

He was glad to see that he still had some food left. He stooped to pick it up but when he smelled it he threw it away. The men had even ruined it. Oh why did they do it? He looked for his pack. It was gone. His money and all his clothes were gone. In sheer hopelessness he fell to the ground. Hot tears falling down his face.

"Omne, I am still here," a voice told him. "I will help you!"

"I don't know you," Omne said and he resisted the voice. "I have no God," he stormed inwardly. I will make it on my own or die trying.

At last his tears were all spent and he knew he had to be on his way. Rising again to his feet he started down the trail. Though it was now an easy trail to travel on, his pain and despair made the going most difficult. Only sheer determination pushed him on. When he at last reached the first river he stripped his clothes off and bathed in the cool water. It felt good to his bruised body and he was glad to feel new strength flow into his inner most soul.

Dressing, he again started on his way. By the light of the sun he knew it was getting late and he did not want to be out here alone another night.

He arrived at the small village just as the sun was sinking over the western horizon. His strength came stronger as hope rose in his heart.

With haste he did not know he could muster, he pushed on to the house he had been instructed to go to. He tried to knock on the door but in his weakened condition was unable to and fell to the ground with a thud. There he lay motionless. He was found a short while later by a young woman. She stifled a scream and called to her husband who was in back of the house. Quickly the two carried the still form into the house and laid him on a mat. Carefully they took off his clothes and bathed his wounds. Tenderly they bandaged the open wounds and covered him with warm, soft blankets.

He lay still, not moving. Several children walked quietly through the house and stared at the stranger.

"He was badly beaten," said the man. "I would say that he has come a long distance after he was hurt. Probably has not had anything to eat all day. Wait, he is starting to move."

Bending low to the stranger the man said, "You are safe now. We are your friends. We will help you."

Opening his eyes Omne saw a man and a woman looking at him. Slowly he turned his head and surveyed the room he was in. It was simple, with only some sleeping mats on the floor and some storage baskets. He could see cooking pots hanging on the wall. He noted that the room was clean. He tried to get up but groaned as the pain shot through him. At last he whispered, "Where am I? I was told I could find help if I went to a certain house just across the little stream. Could you help me there?"

"You are here," answered the man. "Who told you this?"

"A man who lives over the mountains towards Colosse. I don't remember his name."

You mean you came all the way from Colosse? Through the mountains? That is the long way to get here."

"Yes. I know that! It was a long, hard trail!"

"What happened to you?"

I was sleeping in the mountain like I was told to. I guess I was too near the valley for in the early morning some men beat me while I was sleeping. They robbed me of all I had. Even spoiled the little food I had left. Oh I am so tired and sore."

"Here, have some cool water. Drink all of it. Then rest a few minutes and we will feed you. That is good," he said after Omne had drank deeply. "now rest a bit."

When Omne again opened his eyes it was dark out. The children were already lying on their sleeping mats.   Slowly he tried to sit up.   He stifled a groan and then he felt a strong hand behind him, helping him to sit up.

"There, is that better?   Ready for some hot stew?"

"Oh that does sound good."

Carefully the man helped Omne eat.   It was slow as Omne was so sore.   The stew was very good and at last Omne had eaten all he wanted.   "Would you help me stand up?"

"Are you sure you want to try that."

"Yes, I need to stand up; I need to go outside for a bit."

"Okay, I will help you.   Take it slow.

Good, that is the way.   Now just stand for a moment.   Better?   You are doing fine.   Now put your arm around my shoulder and lean on me.   Let me help carry your weight as we walk.   That is fine."

The cool night air fell gently across Omne's body and soul as the men left the warmth of the house.

He slept little that night for he hurt so much. He was not afraid for his life now; it was just that he had so many sores.   Often when he turned, he would moan out.   He would try to muffle his moan but many times he would sense that the man was beside him.   Several times the man spoke quietly to him.   "It will be better soon.   One day at a time. You will make it."

Omne wondered just where he had heard this before.   "One day at a time."   Where was it?   Who used to say it?   As morning light started to show on the Eastern sky, a thought entered his mind. Amil.   That is who used to say "One day at a time." How long had it been?   He could not remember. "Let's see," he mused to himself.   "I was only 15 when I was taken.   Now I am 33 years old.   So that would be 18 years ago.   I wonder what Amil is doing now.   Where is he?   Still a slave?"

This musing was interrupted by the man asking, "How are you?   Do you feel any better this morning?"

"I am very sore and stiff. But thanks to you I am much better. Was it only yesterday that I came? It seems ages since I left your friend in the hills. It was a long night."

"Let me help you into your clothes. They are clean and dry."

"Clean and dry, who washed them?"

"My wife did. She said you could not put those dirty clothes on over all your sores."

"You are both too good to me."

"No, we are not too good. Only doing what the LORD wants us to do."

"You sound like others I know. What does the LORD have to do with you being good?"

"He has everything to do with it."

Here Omne noted that the man was looking at him strangely. Omne looked back at the man. His eyes searched the other man's face. Suddenly a mixture of fear and hope flashed across his face. "Amil!" he gasped out, "Is that really you?" He shook his head as if to clear it and then whispered, "You are my friend Amil?"

"It is you! I thought it was you. But it was so hard to tell last night with all of your bruises. It has been a long time, my friend."

"It has indeed been a long time," replied Omne.

"Tell me about yourself. What has been happening to you, Omne?"

"No, tell me about yourself. Amil I want to hear all about you. How did you get here?"

"Two years after you were taken away I was sold to a man who lives in this village. He never treated me as a slave, but as a son. He had no children and I was like a son to him. No one here, except he, his wife and my wife, know I was ever a slave. I am a free man. Life is good to me. This man knew one called Jesus. Jesus was the Son of God. But wicked people killed him. Still he is alive as he rose from the dead. Well the one who bought me had been with Jesus and saw how kind he was to everyone. Thus he wants to live like he did. He does not like slavery and would abolish it if he could. He is like a father to me. We love him. Our children know him as Grandfather. His wife is like he is. She is so nice. You will have to meet them. I know you will like them. Now what about yourself?"

   "Maybe later. It is not as happy as your life has been."

CHAPTER 7

Omne stayed many days with Amil and his family.
He would often visit with Amil's "parents" too. He
found them just as nice as Amil had said. They
treated him as a member of their own family.

One day as he was talking to Amil, Amil again
brought up the question of Omne's trouble. "Omne,
for you to heal, you must forget and forgive. You
can not carry your burden forever; it will eat at
your soul and destroy you. It will help to talk
about it. For days now you have been avoiding the
subject. Why? Am I not your friend? Do you not
trust me?"

"I trust you, my friend. Why wouldn't I?"

"Then why not tell me all about it?"

"Okay." Omne started at the time he was taken
away from Amil. He told of his new home, family
and loss of his first born son. Here he broke down
and sobbed. He told of his stealing from his
master and his running away. "Now you see, I am
lost. I am no good. How could I do these evil
things to those who love me so?"

"Do you still love your wife?"

"Oh yes."

"Why don't you go back? Your master will
forgive you if he is as good as you say."

"I can't. But I wish I could find a man who
once came to my master's place. He was a man of

God. Maybe he could help me. But no, I am beyond his help too."

"What was his name?"

"That doesn't matter now."

"Was he by any chance called Paul?"

"No that was not his name, but he was a friend of Paul."

"I don't know where Paul is right now. The Jews were trying to trap him so they could have him put to death. I haven't heard about him for some time now."

"How far is it to Troas?"

"Troas? Why? You don't plan to go there do you?"

"Why not? I can't go home. Can't you see that?"

"No I can't. You are making a great mistake. You tell me of your love for your wife and children. You have mentioned how kind your master is, yet you refuse to go home. I don't understand this action. Is your hatred of God that strong?"

"I just don't know what to do. I do miss my wife and children but I can't go back. I have committed too much wrong to ever return," and Omne turned away from his friend feeling the total dejection which filled him leaving no room for anyone or anything else.

Two days later Omne came to Amil and said, "I am leaving in the morning. I am going to Troas. From there I don't know now. Maybe I will stay there."

"If you won't go home why not stay here? We will help you get set up here. Don't go my friend."

"I have to. I must leave soon."

"How will you go?"

"I talked to some merchants who are leaving in the morning. I understand it is a hard trip with many dangers, but I can do it. At least from here to Troas I will not be alone."

"You have no money. What will you do for food?"

"I will get by. I have a plan."

"Your mind is made up then?"

"Yes."

"Well the least we can do is to send a large lunch with you."

Omne left at sun up in the morning. It was a sad parting as his friends did not want to see him leave. The last words he heard as he left was Amil's. "My friend, you can return here anytime. You will always be welcome here. God will go with you. Please lean on him again as in days past. He will not forsake you."

The trip to Troas was long. Fortunately the men he traveled with were honest and he suffered no evil. He shared his lunch with them and in turn they shared theirs with him.

It was a long, hard trip and often at night as he tried to sleep he would toss and turn as his sore muscles reminded him of the difficult trail. He would dream of home and again see Martha. She was always smiling. He would wake up, shaking in fear and frustration. One night he dreamed he was holding her close to him, savoring her closeness to his weary body, only to wake up and feel the total desolation of his loneliness. "Oh why can't I forget her? But do I really want to forget her?" And so he argued with himself.

Once he reached Troas he was on his own. He had no money, his clothes were wearing out. As he heard his stomach growling and felt the weakness coming on, he knew he had to get food. Troas was a busy sea port city. From here one could journey to all points of Asia, Greece and on to Italy and west. He was so sure he could fine work here that for sometime he forgot about the many ships that came and went out of the harbor. But as the day grew later and still he had no work or food he turned towards the seashore. He really had no desire to board a ship. To him they looked ugly and loathsome, but he had to find work soon.

At last he heard of a ship that was leaving for Cyprus. They needed more help and he hired on as a mop boy. He started work that very afternoon. It was after dark before he was allowed to stop. Even

though he was so tired and near collapsing from
lack of food, he had a terrible time getting the
awful tasting food down. He thought of the good
food that Martha always had for him, Also the good
food he had when at Amil's. Well he had run away
from it all. He had to eat what food there was, as
bad as it was, and forget the good food from his
other life.

The day after the ship left port was even worse.
The wind became violent and the ship rocked and
heaved as the waves grew larger and larger. For
awhile it was feared that the ship and all on board
would be lost. Crewmen became sick and their vomit
was all over the decks. Omne had to clean it up
and if the ship master saw any of it he was yelled
at and threatened with the strap. He did his best,
but often had to go to the side of the ship where
the food he had eaten earlier flowed into the sea.
He grew weaker as the days went by. Finally on the
6th day the sea grew calm. With the calmness came
relief for the crew and even Omne began to feel
better.

Now there was fear of being lost at sea with no
wind to fill the sails, but after a few hours of
calm, the wind started up, filling the sails and
the ship began to move.

Because of the delay caused by the storm the
food supply ran low. If the food was bad before,
it was even worse now. Still the men had no other
choice but to eat what there was.

"Land! I see land!" came the cry from the look
out perched high up in the sails. With joy the men
prepared to make harbor.

That evening Omne stood on solid ground. He
clutched the money, his wages, in a fold of his
garment.

The pay was not much but it would last him for
awhile. He planned to get a job here on Cyprus.
It was a nice place to stay with many warm days and
cool nights. Day by day he searched for a job.
His money ran low and still no job. Would he have
to go on ship again? "Never," he vowed.

64

At last he found a job in a copper mine. It was hard work but at least he had food to eat and a hut to sleep in. The hours were long usually lasting from sun-up to about an hour before sundown. He had one day off a week and on these he would search out the wonders of his new home.

Still, even with the long hard hours of work and his weariness at days end, he was unable to get Martha and the children out of his mind. Often during the night he would wake up, bathed in sweat with his heart pounding. Again he had seen her running away from him. She would not come to him no matter how he pleaded. "Oh, can I never forget?"

He was strolling near the waterfront one day when he heard two men talking. He was sure he knew one of the men and he walked slower to listen. Yes, now he knew who it was. Had they seen him, did they remember him? The voice was that of one of the bandits who had years before captured him. He could never forget that voice. It was the man who had been the most cruel to him. Even now Omne shuddered as he remembered.

"I must leave this area right away," he said to himself as he hurried back to his shelter.

He never stopped to rationalize that after the many years that had past it was doubtful that the bandits would recognize him for then he was a lad and now he was a man. "As soon as I get my next pay I will leave." Then he paused in his flight to consider his options. "If I leave here I must get on a ship again! Can I stand it?" he wondered.

The very next day Omne went in search of a ship leaving port. He was directed to a rather old looking ship rocking gently on the waves.

"Yes this ship is leaving in 2 days. Yes we need more help."

"Where is the ship headed?"

"It is taking a load to be delivered to the Centurion in Rome. It will dock at the port city of Puteoli. From there the cargo will have to be transported overland to Rome." The man studied

Omne as he spoke. "Are you looking for a job? I could use another hand on board."

"Yes," Omne replied. "I was hoping to go to Rome."

Omne was hired. This time he helped in the galley and cleaned up after the meals. Again it was hard, long work, but this time his master was not so hot-headed. Omne had little free time, but at least he had good food and the trip was not a rough passage. Still he was very glad to get his feet on land again.

Puteoli was a bustling port city on the sea coast of Italy. Omne was allowed 3 days there while more men were hired to help transport the cargo to Rome. He soon discovered that this city, too, was an evil one. Once when he was out on the streets too late in the evening he was clubbed from behind and robbed. He woke up two hours later, lying in the road, no one to help him. His head ached as he made his way to his room. Fortunately, most of his money had been left in his room. But it was not so well for him the next night.

Yes, he was lonely. He had been away from Martha for several months now and he felt so all alone. He was wandering down a street when a lovely young lady approached him. He was not used to life in the city and was not prepared for its wild life. He was so lonely and this woman was so pleasant to be with. For awhile they sat on a small bench and talked. She too was lonely. He was captivated with her smile and dancing eyes which sparkled in the dying light. Without realizing it he was drawn to a shabby room where she pulled him to her. He had no strength to resist and like an ox going to water, he gave in to her desires. Only later did he realize what he had done. Still he reasoned, "I am alone now. Why not enjoy life."

It was near day-break when he entered his room and began to get ready for the trip to Rome. He was tired and fumed with himself for his wild night. But he was more upset when he felt for his money pouch. It was gone. All of it. He slowly awoke to the realization of what had happened.

Well there was nothing he could do now. He could get 2 hours sleep, then he would have to go to the dock and get his load ready. "It is going to be a long, hard trip," he muttered to himself. "Will I make it?"

There were 15 horse drawn wagons, all heavily laden, 25 donkeys with packs on their backs. Not only were they taking the supplies to be delivered in Rome but they had to carry enough food for the animals and workers. It was a large caravan that headed towards Rome that day. It would be a long overland trip, lasting 2 or more weeks with a motley bunch of workers that were helping. Many were slaves and these also carried packs, some on their heads, others on their backs. Omne was not required to carry a pack. His job on the trip was to help watch the slaves and keep them in order. Having been a slave for years, though no one there knew that fact, Omne was more sympathetic with the treatment of the slaves than were most of the other guards. Often a slave was whipped for the slightest mistake. Once a slave was severely beaten for tripping on a stone. He stumbled but did not fall, still he was beaten. The guard was so angry that he would have killed the slave had not Omne intervened. As the guard stormed away, Omne helped soothed the slave. Yet there was little else he dared do. If he were not careful he himself would be in trouble.

For two long and grueling days they continued, stopping only for meals and a few hours of rest at night.

On the morning of the third day the head master of the pack train came to Omne. "Omne," he said, "I have noticed that the slaves under your control do much better then the others do. I don't know if you have realized it or not, but twice I have taken troublesome slaves out of other groups and added them to your group. They are well behaved for you. I have also taken some of your best slaves and given them to another slave-driver and he has much trouble with them. Why is this?"

"Sir, the slaves are also people. How would you react if you were beaten for the smallest thing and were never praised for good work? Would you not rebel too?"

"I never thought of it that way. But you are right. Do you have any suggestions?"

"How many slaves do we have with us?"

"I think we have 55 slaves and 5 slave drivers."

"Sir, how do the slaves act when in the group that Simon has? I think he also treats them fair."

"That is true. He doesn't have any trouble either. Why do you ask?"

"Well sir, why not let Simon and I work with all the slaves, divide them between the two of us."

"I will see about that but that will be a lot of slaves for just one man to watch. I must check with Simon first."

"I am making some changes," the pack train master said as they were getting ready for the days trip. "I want all of you here for a minute. From now on Omne and Simon will be in charge of all the slaves."

"Hey, wait a minute," shouted one of the slave drivers. "That is not right!"

"You," and the master looked at the man with anger shooting out from his eyes, "and those two standing with you are the very men who are causing the trouble with the slaves. You beat them for no reason at all. You three will now help the ones in charge of the donkeys. See if you can control them. I will not listen to any arguments over this. Is that clear?"

"Yes," all answered.

That morning all went much smoother for the pack train. That is except for one incident.

Omne had his group of slaves on one side of the pack train and Simon had his on the other side. Now one of the men who used to be a slave-driver was helping with the donkeys. This man was near the slaves and would make his donkey swerve into the slaves near him. Omne and Simon noted this but trying to avoid trouble they instructed their slaves to stay farther away from the donkeys. Both men kept an eye on the trouble maker. He still would try to run his donkey into the line of slaves. Then it happened again. But this time the master saw what had happened.

He also noted that this time the slave that was bumped by the donkey was hurt. Immediately he stopped the pack train. Walking over to the trouble maker he pulled him over to where the injured slave was now sitting and said to him, "You have been making trouble for the slaves for a long time. I have seen what you are doing. I also noted that they have tried to stay out of your way but you deliberately run your donkey into them. Well I will teach you a lesson I hope you will never forget. You are to take the load from the injured man and you are to now carry it. You will carry it for the rest of the day while the slave rides in a cart to rest. Tomorrow if the slave is well enough to carry his load, you will be released to go where you want to. If the slave can't yet carry his load you will carry it until the day he can resume his load. Then you will go your way. I do not need the likes of you working for me. Now pick up that load so we can be on our way."

Angrily the man picked up the load. After the master had the injured man resting in a cart he returned to where he could watch the slaves, as he wanted to see what the ex-slave-driver would do. This man was in Omne's group and his anger showed on his face all day. It was also soon clear that the man was not used to doing hard work. Towards late afternoon he was stumbling and nearly fell several times, and would have if Omne had not caught him.

The man nearly collapsed on the ground when at last they stopped for the night. After camp was set up Omne came to the new slave. "Here, let me help you. Lie there while I rub this ointment over your sore body. The man started to protest but was too weak to offer much resistance. He lay there as Omne worked out the kinks in his sore muscles. Later Omne brought some food for the man to eat. His master drew him apart from the rest. "Why don't you leave him alone. Look at all the trouble he has caused and still you help him. Why?"

"He is a fellow man. I think he will learn the lesson well. Let him work with me for at least another day. Then you can decide for yourself what to do with the man."

"Okay, if you are sure," the master replied. "But I think you are just asking for trouble with that man; he is just no good. If it were I doing your work, I surely would give him a hard time; but instead you do all you can to help him." Here the man stopped as he studied Omne. "I would be most pleased to have you work for me on every trip I make. You are well worth your wages and as of today your wages will be increased." Before Omne could protest the master went to the new slave. He said, "Thomas, the slave is not ready to carry his load yet. You will have to carry it another day."

Though Thomas was still angry, he was to tired to make any protest. Also he was starting to think a little. "What was there about Omne that made him different from the rest?

Omne did his work well and treated his slaves well to. And after all I have done, Omne still treats me with care. In fact I wonder if it was not even Omne's intervening in my behalf for me even having the job yet. Still I think I will test him again tomorrow. But for now all I want to do is to get some rest."

The next day started out without incident. At first the new slave tried to act tired. He stumbled often and at times would limp. Omne would encourage him to keep up and even help him at times by letting the man lean on him. By early afternoon Thomas had his answer. He settled down to the task. Though he was indeed very tired, and his every muscle cried out with pain, he carried his load without grumbling or complaining. But when they stopped for the night he dropped under his load. Tenderly Omne removed his load and laid him on his pad. Later when the master came by one look at Omne and then at the man and he had his answer. Turning to Thomas he asked, "How are you tonight? Do you want your fee and go now or in the morning?"

"Sir, if it is okay, can I go on with you. Even as a slave here with Omne is better then going back in disgrace. I was wrong. I did not see the slaves as other people. Please give me another chance and you will see that what I say is now the truth. I will do my work well if you will but give me another try."

"Very well. I will give you another try. But you will be watched closely," answered the master."

In the morning you will again work with the slaves by assisting Omne and Simon with their job. I will be watching you and will not put up with any misbehaving from you. You will be on probation until we get to Rome. If I feel at that time you are worth it I will pay you your full wages. Is that fair? That is if Omne and Simon will accept your help."

Turning to the two men the now contrite man looked pleadingly for an answer.

Smiling, both Omne and Simon said, "It is fine he can work with us."

"It is settled." And the pack train master left to see about other matters.

71

CHAPTER 8

The new slave-driver proved he was a new man. No longer did he abuse the slaves. He was considerate of all his fellow workers and stopped exploding over the smallest infraction or minor disagreements. He worked diligently, always doing his full share and would often be seen helping another carry his heavy burden. He offered encouragement to the slaves, lifting not only their physical burdens but helping them cope with their mental burdens. The slaves began turning to him for counsel and would seek him out when a problem occurred.

The head master watched from the sideline and shook his head in amazement. "Omne," he said, "What have you done to Thomas? I can't believe the change in him. He is becoming one of my best workers. What did you do to him?"

Omne smiled and replied, "he has changed hasn't he? I can trust him with whatever job I give him. I am happy that you are pleased with him now."

"Pleased with him? I am most grateful to you and Simon for convincing me to give him another chance." Then shaking his head he added, "I don't know what you did but keep up the good work. You three will have a job with me for every trip if you want. I need more trusted workers like you."

Omne considered what the head master had said. "It seems I can't change even when I try."

"I try to run away from God but he stays nearby and helps when I need him, even though I don't ask him. Am I never alone?"

One evening after camp was set up Thomas came to where Omne and Simon were sitting, resting under a tree. Trees were rare in this part of the land and they were enjoying its late evening shade. "Omne, you and Simon work and talk like the followers of the Christ who they say rose from the dead. Are you, for if you are I would like to know more about him."

"I was but not any more. He let me down," Omne said."

"I am," said Simon," as he looked intently at Omne. Then turning to Thomas he said, "I will be glad to tell you all I know. Christ, also called Jesus, was the LORD of all. He showed the Jews where they were wrong in their teaching and this made the Jewish leaders mad. A few accepted the truth but most would not. They crucified the LORD. But, as had been prophesied many years ago, Jesus arose on the third day. Many saw him and later witnessed him as he was taken to Heaven. He taught that all men were equal and should live peaceably together. He showed that the Sabbath was made for man and was to be a day of joy. The Jews had made it a day of frustration and boredom by their many traditions. They had so many restrictions for that day that the Sabbath, meant to be a blessing, became a curse to the Jews. But why do you think I am one of them?"

"You are kind. You help everyone. You look for the good in people and try to bring the good out. You are a fair boss. Omne is also the same and even if he says he is no longer a follower of this one called Jesus, I can tell he still is. I am so happy that I was made to work with you for now I want to learn more about your God. I used to think he was a phony but after seeing his religion in work I can see that he was, and indeed still is, the true God. I shudder to think what might have happened to me if it wasn't for the two of you,

especially Omne, for I think it was he who
convinced the master to give me another chance. My
life was a mess; I was on the road of self-
destruction when you stopped me in my tracks."
Here he stopped, a frown crossing his face as he
remembered the past.

Continuing, Thomas said, "Yes, I have Omne to
thank for literally saving my life. I have not
told anyone this but if it wasn't for him I would
no longer be alive."

"Just what are you saying," Omne asked. His
face wore a look of shock and fear.

"Well," Thomas continued, "That day I ran the
donkey into the slave and injured him was a dark
day for me. Inwardly I was boiling mad I was angry
at the master and mad at the two of you.

I blamed the two of you for the master making me
a donkey driver. Now don't look so shocked for I
am sure you could feel my anger towards you. I
began looking for a way that I could kill the
master and get away with his money."

A short gasp escaped Omne's throat as he stared
at Thomas.

"I am sure I could never have done this and I
probably would have been killed on the spot. But I
still fumed inside and considered my plans while
all along I tried to make life miserable for Omne.
I was not in good physical condition due to my wild
living. I grew so tired as I struggled to carry
that heavy pack and wondered how anyone could carry
it all day without falling under its load. As the
day progressed and my strength failed, I began to
think of ways to kill myself. Then just when I
thought I could go no farther Omne came and helped
me carry the load. I was too amazed and tired to
even react against his kind offer. Then after we
stopped for the night he rubbed soothing ointment
over my sore, taunt muscles and brought me food,
insisting I eat it. I still think it was all
Omne's doings that convinced the master to even let
me go on," and here he looked over at Omne. "I
have the feeling that the injured slave was indeed

ready to carry his load the next day but somehow Omne saw hope for me if I carried the load one more day."

When neither Omne or Simon replied, Thomas smiled and said, "I thought so, and I am grateful for this chance. This is why I want to learn more about this Jesus for your lives have been such a blessing to me. When I get to Rome I want to look up a man. He was a true follower of Christ, his life being a witness to his faith."

"Thomas, do you remember this man's name?"

"His name was Paul. I remember him well for I was on the ship with him when he was taken to Rome. The Jews had tried to kill him and he was going under guard to Caesar. I thought he was odd, but he was the one who saved all of our lives."

"Saved all of your lives? How did he do that?"

"Well first he tried to convince the captain of the ship to stay in the harbor, where we were, for the winter. He said there would be great loss if we left. But no one wanted to stay there as the town was small and there was nothing exciting to do there."

"You were pleased when the captain decided to set sail?"

"Oh yes, I was excited for I had heard of the 'fun' I could have in the next port. I yearned for the wild life and looked forward to landing in that large port city.

Well, a storm came up. I have been in many storms but never one like this. It struck at night and the first I knew of it was when I was pitched out of my bunk onto the hard floor. The ship rocked and pitched in the mountainous waves; the wind howled and the thunder crashed violently. The ship creaked and groaned in the storm's fury and I just knew that my wild life was over. We would all be buried on the bottom of the sea! We threw the cargo overboard to lighten the ship in hope of saving our lives. Still the storm grew worse. We were frantic and near despair; each man praying to his own god. Some of us were beating our chests, others were cutting themselves in an attempt to prove their need to their god. In our fear we became violent and many fights arose. Instead of banding together and trying to think of ways to save our lives we turned against each other"

"Then the captain found Paul asleep on his bed. He asked, 'why are you here sleeping? Don't you know that the ship is going down? We will all be lost. Say, maybe you are the cause of our trouble. Why are you here? Get up and pray to your god.'

Now listen to this. This is what Paul said.

'Sir, I told you not to leave that harbor we were in and you would not heed my instructions. I warned you of the danger to our lives, cargo and to the ship but you would not listen to me. You laughed at me and said I was crazy. You told me that you knew more about the sea then I did. Remember that? Now you are seeking my help? It is past time to pray. But look here my man, don't fret so. Not one soul on board will be lost if you follow my instructions now."

'No man will be lost?' the captain shouted back, trying to be heard above the roar of the wind and the creaks and groans of the faltering ship. 'The ship is sinking and you say no one will be lost. Man, you are crazy!'

'Listen to what I say and no one will be lost,' replied Paul. 'First have everyone eat. You have not eaten for 2 days and you will need your strength for the coming trial. Now set food before the men and eat.' With this Paul took food and started to eat. Seeing him eating, the other men began to eat too."

"Before light the next morning we heard breakers and fearful of hitting rocks the anchors were lowered. Then it was discovered that the sailors were letting the life rafts down in an attempt to escape for their lives and abandon ship."

"When Paul heard this he shouted, 'if the sailors or anyone abandons the ship all on board, plus those attempting to escape will be lost.'

Hearing this, the soldiers rushed to the sides of the ship where the rafts were even then being lowered into the stormy water. The soldiers cut the ropes and the life rafts fell empty into the water below."

At first light, we could see land and lifting the anchors we sped for the narrow harbor. But we struck the rocks and the ship began to break up. The soldiers wanted to kill the prisoners but the head guard wanted to spare Paul. 'No one is to be killed was the order,' he shouted. 'Everyone is to jump into the water and head to shore. Use boards or whatever you can find to get there.'

"Well, strange as it may be, Paul was right. Not a person perished."

"This really happened?"

"Yes it did. And there is more. There were people living on the island where we landed. They helped us get a fire going so we could get warm and dry our clothes. While Paul was gathering wood he was bitten by a viper. Everyone expected to see him drop dead soon as it was very poisonous but he had no adverse trouble at all. No pain, no swelling, he just brushed it into the fire and went on as if nothing had happened."

"How can that be? You are just making up a big story," and Simon looked with concern at Thomas.

"This is not a story I made up. It did happen just the way I told you. It was enough to change anyone's hard heart but I refused to consider that a miracle had happened."

"I have heard of this Paul but don't know him. I would like to see him. Do you know where he is?" asked Simon.

"Not for sure but the last I knew he was still in Rome. He is in prison still I think. They know he is not guilty of any wrong yet they still keep him there. I think that even the Romans are afraid of the Jews."

"I once saw a close follower of Paul's," spoke up Omne. He stayed with friends of mine many years ago. He spoke of this Paul and taught us many

77

things about this Christ that you talk about. If Paul is like this man, then I too would like to see him. Maybe he can help me."

Thomas looked at Omne. "I can see you are troubled. I thought it was because of your hatred of the suffering you see all around, but now I wonder if it is not more serious. Hey, why don't the three of us try to find Paul? We will have several days, maybe several weeks even, in Rome before we need to return to the port."

"Yes, Simon answered immediately. It will also be safer for us if we are together and not alone in that great city." They turned to look at Omne.

"Sure! But it is getting late and we will need our sleep."

Rain was falling as the caravan started on its way the next morning. The rain continued for two days, which made traveling very difficult for man and beast. Though most of the road was made of inlaid rock, some of the donkeys and the slaves had to walk in the slippery mud of the road's shoulders. Occasionally an ox cart would slip off the rocks, sinking into the soft mud. Mud soon covered everything and everyone. Tempers flared and fights erupted frequently. No one trusted anyone else. Yet the three slave leaders remained calm and in control. The slaves were encouraged and helped as needed. In fact there was less trouble with them than with the donkey drivers, especially between two of them. Finally the master had to separate the two and the trip was more peaceful for a few miles.

"Omne," said Thomas quietly as he walked beside his new friend, "watch out for those two donkey drivers."

"Why?"

"Thomas looked at Omne for a long moment before he answered. "Don't you remember? They are the other two slave drivers who were made to be donkey drivers. They were just as cruel to the slaves as I was! They blame each other for their misery and their anger is boiling over.

May I stay on this side with you. I do not feel safe near them. I fear they might take out their revenge on me. I see them glaring in my direction and their looks bother me. I do not want to be in a fight. I am sure I could defend myself against them but do not want to cause any distrust in the master's mind about my ability to do my work well."

"Alright, you help with the slaves here and I will assist with them farther back. Keep your eyes open and be on the guard; I will do the same. I think the master is also watching them closely now. They are full of anger; it is plain to see."

Late in the afternoon on the second day of rain the caravan came to a stream. This stream was usually a small trickle, a cool oasis along the dusty road, an easy one to cross. But this day it was a raging demon, thrashing and foaming in its anger as it tore at its banks in an effort to free itself.

The order was given to set up camp and wait until morning. It was hoped the rain would stop and the raging river would return to its normal flow. With much cursing and shoving, the men tried to find spots that weren't soft mud to set their tents on. There were few of these places and most had to settle for the less desirable spots. There was little sleep that night as it was nearly impossible to stay dry.

Day light found the rain still falling. The stream was still thrashing in its fury. But by the time they had eaten their morning meal the rain had stopped and the sun was peeping out over the soggy land.

"We will stay here today. We can get dried out and maybe the stream will be easier to cross in the morning," said the master.

The trouble of the day before was forgotten, at least by most of them. But not by all. The two donkey drivers were still angry. Suddenly there was a shout. All turned to see the two fighting. They were slugging each other and then they were in the mud thrashing out with legs and fists. They rolled and splashed around in the mud never realizing how close they were getting to the raging river. One of the two stood up and was about to kick the other man when the man on the ground gave a hard kick to the other man's low belly. With a shout of pain the man doubled over as the pain racked his whole body. Undaunted with the man's pain, the man who was still lying in the mud gave another kick, this time catching his opponent on his leg, toppling him into the water. For a moment no one moved. Then several of the men rushed to the water's side to search for the man. They saw him once away down the stream as he was thrown about like a small boat in a raging sea. That was the last he was seen.

Standing up, the other man came face to face with the train master. Anger shot out of the master's eyes as he glared at the mud covered man. "Well now you are a mess. And thanks to you we are now short a donkey driver. Maybe you will cool down as you guide two donkeys. I should have sent you on your way when I changed your job from slave driver to donkey driver. You have been angry all the way and a trouble-maker. Now you will have to keep both your donkey and the other man's donkey under control for the remainder of the journey. Maybe this will keep you out of trouble!"

"Both! How do I control both donkeys at the same time?" the man sputtered.

"I would say that you had just better find a way for there is no one else to do it."

All day the men washed and cleaned their clothes and bedding. The wagons were wiped off and all supplies were checked and sorted and re-packed. By nightfall the men were in better spirits and the camp was quieter. It promised to be a better day tomorrow and they were anxious to get to Rome. Already they had lost 2 days, and they did not want to lose any more time.

The next morning dawned clear, with a hope of fair weather. The muddy river was calmer and was running smoothly. Though still flowing deeper than it usually did The order was given to make ready to move. Excitement reigned as the men loaded their burdens and broke up camp. Even the beasts of burden appeared eager to be on their way. Crossing the stream helped to clean the mud off the wagons and all emerged on the other side cleaner. They hoped they could reach Rome in five more days.

That evening after the men had set up camp, Thomas said, "You know, Omne, you remind me of another man I met some time ago. He looked a lot like you and was also very kind. He was with us when we brought in more horses for the Emperor. I wonder where he is now."

"How old was he? Do you have a name for him?"

"Well let me see. I think he would be near your age and his name was David."

"Did he talk about his home?"

"Yes, he said his home was in a small village about 2 or 3 hard days travel from Colosse I believe."

"Did he talk of a family?"

"Only that he still lived at home and he had several siblings. He also spoke of Paul. Maybe that is why I again thought of him. He was quiet, not a trouble maker and was anxious to get back home. But since he was this far he hoped he could first see Paul. At the time I thought him strange as he was so quiet and did not do any of the wild things that I enjoyed."

"Why was he here?"

"Oh he said he had wanted to get away and see the world. But the world he saw was not a good one. He said he now could go home and be satisfied with life there. I think there was a girl there who he was very interested in too."

Omne was thoughtful for awhile. "Could he be my brother? No," he reasoned, "Probably not. Still it might be worth looking into." The thought of his parents and family brought again that old homesickness to his soul.

"I wonder how they are. How I would like to see them and tell them I am okay. But am I okay?" he

thought. "Here I am running away from those I love
and who love me. How could I have done this to
them? Well it is too late now. They would not
want me back now even if I returned. And my
master, kind as he was, would probably put me in
chains if I return now. No, I can never return
home. But maybe I can go see my parents. Maybe
when I am through here in Rome I will try to find
them," he thought.

At last they reached the large city of Rome.
They went immediately to deliver the supplies. The
pack train master said that he would be here for 3
weeks. After all the goods were delivered he paid
the men their wages. He told them to be back in 3
weeks if they wanted to travel back with him. He
made a point of speaking to Omne, Simon and Thomas,
"I will be pleased if you three want to help me on
the return trip."

Simon, Thomas and Omne had already decided to
stay together as it was safer that way. What lay
ahead would be something that no one could have
expected. They were to discover just what a city
of this magnitude could hold for them; and what it
could give to or take away from those in its grasp.

CHAPTER 9

The men rented a small, but very clean room on the roof of a house situated on the edge of the city. There were steps going up the outside of the house to enter the room.

"I will prepare meals for you too if you let me know ahead of time when you wish to eat with us," said the lady of the house.

Thanking her the three men said that for now they had some food with them and would probably be eating in town most of the time. "But we sure do appreciate your kind offer," Simon replied for the three men. "It does sound good and we will let you know early if we choose to eat with you."

That first afternoon and night they stayed in their room or walked about in the courtyard. This courtyard was surrounded with a stone wall that was about 6 feet tall. This offered much privacy from the neighbors houses. It was secluded, in a quiet area away from the noise and bustle of the city. After the long and stressful trip they were thankful to just relax. They went to their sleeping mats early for a sound night's sleep.

The next morning they left right after they had finished eating. They planned to be in their room before nightfall, for they had no desire for Rome's night-life. The city appeared more tranquil, more peaceful in the morning but they knew this could be deceiving! They passed the great arena and heard the screams and shouts of the crowd there, but did not stop.

They entered a little open air food stand and ordered their meal. As they ate they watched the throng of people who seemed to be always in a hurry. They saw men of all colors and nationalities, each jostling with the others as they strove to reach their destination.

That afternoon, while on their way back to their room, they noted a large group of men standing in a plaza ahead of them. Wondering what was the commotion, they walked towards the men. Suddenly, sensing that they might be walking into danger, Thomas said quietly, "We had better get out of here. Slowly turn to the right and walk down that lane. Do not hurry nor look over your shoulders." Thomas stiffen as he and the others walked away from the crowd.

"What was wrong back there? Why did you tell us to leave and to leave in the direction you led us? It appeared to be the long way home." Omne asked as soon as they had entered their courtyard. "Just what was the problem? The men looked harmless to me."

"I am really not sure but I felt we would be in grave danger if we continued on our way towards them. Remember, this is a wicked city. Care is of the upmost importance," Thomas answered, still shaken. "It was if someone told me to leave and to go the way we did."

The next day they again searched through the great city. But already the three were growing tired of what they found. It was so noisy with the crowd always pushing and shoving. In the city the air was heavy with the odors of animals, people, food and fires.

"I am about ready to leave this city," Simon said as they walked along. "But where do we go? It is still over two weeks until we can go back with the pack train. I don't like it. I feel so uneasy as if danger is stalking us."

"I too am tired of this life here. Part of it pulls at me to join in and the other part of me is constantly at war with this old desire. I can never be happy in a city like this again," spoke up Thomas.

The three walked along in silence for a few minutes as they struggled with their own inner feelings. Suddenly they were brought back to the present when another man joined them. "Mind if I walk along with you?" the stranger asked. His voice was pleasant and his eyes were bright with friendliness. It could also be readily seen that he was a visitor too.

Quickly Thomas answered, "Not at all, you are welcomed. Where are you from and what are you doing here?"

"Oh I am just visiting here too. I have a friend who is held captive here and I do all I can to help him." He talked easily and well in their own language. "Where are you men from?" he asked.

"We hail from different places," Thomas answered.

"I am Tychicus. I am from Macadonia. I plan to go to Colosse soon."

"I am from Colosse, or I used to live there," said Omne. "Will you be here long?"

"I don't know. I will not leave until there is more help for my friend."

"Who is this friend of yours. He must be a grand friend for you to be so devoted to him."

"He is a wonderful friend. He does not belong in prison, actually he is just under guard and lives in a small house near the prison. I am on my way to see him now. Want to go with me? His name is Paul."

"Paul!" all three chorused. Then Simon added, "The Paul, the great apostle of one named Jesus Christ?"

"That is he. Do you know him too?"

Simon answered, "I do not know him but have heard much about him and the good he does. I too believe."

"So do I now," added Thomas. I was on a ship with Paul once. There was a bad ship wreck and it was thanks to Paul that no one was lost."

"Was that the time he ship-wrecked on the Island of Malta?"

"Yes, I was a worker on that ship."

"And you?" he asked looking at Omne. "Do you know Paul?"

"No I don't know Paul. But one of his friends stopped at my place when he was in Colosse. But that was a long time ago."

"I see," said the stranger. "Well here we are. We can go right in as he will be expecting me. He will welcome you too."

They entered a doorway into a small house. Inside, the house was neat and clean. A gentle breeze came through the open windows. The room itself was bright and cheery. Paul was sitting on a hard stool near a window and writing on a scroll.

Turning, as the men entered, Paul spoke, "Tychicus, you are back and who do you have here. You always find someone to bring home. You are a good missionary."

"Paul, please meet Thomas, Simon and Omne.

"Welcome my friends. May God Bless you. What brings you to Rome."

Simon spoke up, "We helped bring a load here from the coast. Now we are visiting the town. I have heard a lot about you sir. I am so glad to get to meet you. I too believe but need to learn much more about Jesus and His work."

"I," spoke up Thomas, "am here due to the good witnessing of these two good men. I once was on a ship with you. It was a bad voyage. You had tried to persuade the captain to not leave the harbor but he would not listen to you. The ship sank near Malta."

"You were on that ship? Come closer so I can see you better. Oh yes, now I remember. You were not too kind to the slaves or prisoners."

Thomas hung his head. "I am ashamed to say that was me. I did not value human life then. But thanks to the example of these two I learned love for all. Please accept my humble apology for I am truly sorry."

"I hold nothing against you. I can see that you are a Christian now."

Omne spoke as Paul turned to face him. "Yes Thomas is a great helper now. Thanks to his quick thinking he might have kept us from grave trouble last night."

"What about you, my friend? You look like one in great distress of mind. I see I will need to have a talk with you. I will try to help you. But first let us eat. I am hungry and I am sure that all of you are too. We will talk later. Also there is another man I want you to meet."

It was a simple meal and the men visited as they ate. Omne began to relax as he listened to the other men talk. He felt drawn to this Paul. He wanted to talk to Paul alone but yet was afraid to do so. How could he, a great sinner, talk to Paul who was a servant of God?

It was late afternoon when Omne said to his friends, "you can stay longer but I think I will go back to our room."

Thomas questioned the wisdom of Omne going alone, "there is danger out there for a stranger alone. Shouldn't you wait for us or we could go now too." He looked at Simon for his response.

"Yes, we can all go now. I too don't like the idea of you being alone on the streets this afternoon." He started to get up but was stopped by Omne.

"There is no reason for the two of you to leave early. It is still several hours before dark and I will be fine. I will meet you in our room later," and with that he left the house. Omne really felt a need to be alone for a few minutes so he could try to sort out his troubled thoughts.

"What do you know about Omne," Paul asked the two men after Omne left the house.

"Very little," replied Simon. "He will not talk about his life. He is good to everyone and will help anyone in need but speaks nothing of his past."

"I don't know any more than what Simon has mentioned," said Thomas. "But it is mostly because of him that I am what I am today. He really saved my life and with Simon's help, has turned me about face. He is in distress but hides it from all, while at the same time he helps those in need. I feel he is deeply troubled and needs our help and prayers."

"Pray for him and be his friend," spoke Paul. "He needs you. Let us pray for him right now for I am most concerned for his welfare. I feel he is in grave danger right now!"

The men visited for about an hour after Omne left, with much of the conversation being about Omne.

Omne set off in a brisk walk, taking what He hoped was the shortest way to his room. He was so deep in thought that he paid little attention to his surroundings. Had he paid more attention, he would have realized that he was headed for trouble. Suddenly he bumped into someone. Startled he said, "Please excuse me. I did not see you. Guess I was not watching where I was going."

The man was a large man and as Omne looked at him he noted several more men standing with him. His heart rate increased as he saw the danger he was in. Well maybe, he thought, they are friendly. I will try that approach anyway. "It is a nice, warm day today isn't it?"

"Yes it is. Where are you from and what are you doing here?" The man spoke slowly as he tried to speak so Omne could understand him.

"I came from Colosse. I helped bring a load of wares here and am now just looking at your town and seeing the sights. I am on my way to my room as it has been a long day."

"Why don't you come with us? Maybe we can help you. We won't keep you long and we will see that you get to your room before dark."

The men seemed friendly but even if they weren't what choice did he have? Still there remained that fear, the feeling that he was in grave danger. He would try to excuse himself again. "I really need to get to my room. If I delay my friends will worry about me. Also I am very tired so please excuse me."

"Not so fast my friend," the man replied while he placed his hand firmly on Omne's shoulder. We will not delay you long. Come and join us for a few minutes. We insist, don't we?" and he turned to his friends.

"Sure we do. You must come with us so we can help you," one of them answered.

Omne tried to remain calm as he answered, "Okay, but I really need to get to my room soon. My friends will be there and will worry about me."

"Just rest with us a few moments and you will be refreshed and feel so much better," the first man answered. Then taking his hand, he led him through the streets, stopping at last in front of a dark, dreary looking building.

"Here we are," said one of the men.

It was dark in the room and it took Omne's eyes a few minutes to adjust to the dim light. He saw other men and women there. Some were sitting at tables, drinking strong wine. "Here," they called, "come join us." Then noticing Omne they added, "Oh, you have a new friend with you. Good, bring him too."

Omne was seated at a table with the other men all around him. Wine was past around and a cup full was set before him. Omne remembered the only time before when he had drank strong wine and hesitated to do so again. As he sat there looking at the sparkling wine someone spoke up. "Drink up my friend. There is more where this came from. It will make you feel good and you can forget all of your troubles."

Omne started to get up. "I really should be on my way. I thank you men for your hospitality. Please excuse me."

"Not so fast my good man," spoke up the man who had brought him there. "These men have offered you a drink of their best. Do not offend them by refusing it."

Sitting down, Omne took a sip. It burned his throat as it went down, but he drank some more and more finally emptying the cup.

Again he started to get up. But this time the man sitting next to him put his hand on Omne's shoulder and gently applied pressure forcing Omne down.

"Here is some more. Isn't it good?"

Already Omne's senses were beginning to dull. He relaxed and started talking freely. Then some women came over and the group started laughing and the talk soon was very loud and course. An inner voice told Omne to leave but he was unable to get up. He started to talk to a beautiful woman who was very close to him. He could feel her presence affecting him and with his foggy mind pressed even closer to her. She was so close to him now and so real. Suddenly he felt a sharp blow to the side of his head. He reeled across the room, shaking his head as he tried to understand just what had happened. He looked for the source of the blow and saw a large, red faced man staring down at him.

Glaring the man said, "That is my woman you are messing with."

Omne was now more alert, the pain causing some of the stupor to evaporate like steam rising in warm, dry air. "I am sorry man. I mean no harm. I think I had better go now. Thank you for the evening."

Omne stood and started on unsteady feet for the door. He thought the floor was spinning and tipping and he struggled to find the door. Just as he was stepping out into the now night air, one of the men who brought him in said, "Wait, it is too far for you to go alone, better go with me. In the morning I will show you the way." And without waiting for Omne to answer he took his arm and they walked out into the night. Fear started to well up

in Omne's heart but he was the man's prisoner and
had to obey. Also he felt like he could not walk
far without help.

Entering a small shed the man gave Omne another
drink and they laid down on sleeping mats, one to
try to sleep off his stupor and the other to wait.

Sometime in the late hours the other man got up
and searched through Omne's clothing. He cursed to
himself when he found little money and no
valuables. Taking what money he found he began
beating the sleeping man. Then as Omne went limp
he tied him securely to a post and went out,
locking the house behind him.

****

"May we return tomorrow and talk to you more?"
Thomas asked Paul as Simon and he stood up to
leave.

"Please come back; I have much to tell you! Be
sure Omne comes too!"

Thomas and Simon hurried in the growing dusk to
their room. They thought they might even over take
Omne but did not see him. Arriving at their room
their worry for Omne increased when they found the
room empty. Talking between themselves they
decided to wait. Omne had said he wanted to be
alone a bit. It grew late and still Omne did not
come, and the men grew more distressed. But they
knew it was not safe to go out and search for him.
Fitfully they slept that night. Often waking up
they would offer another prayer for his safety.

Morning came at last and still no Omne. As soon
as they could get ready they went to see Paul.
Tychicus answered the door to their urgent
knocking. He looked at the two, standing there
before him, obviously very troubled. "Why whatever
is the matter. Please come in. Paul, Thomas and
Simon are here to see you."

"Welcome, so good to see you again. Can I help
you."

"Sir, Omne is missing. He did not come home last night. What shall we do?"

"Have you seen him since he left here yesterday afternoon?"

"No, that is the problem. Omne would not just leave without saying anything. Besides, all his things are still in the room. We talked to the owners of the house and they have not seen him either. I have a feeling they know everything that goes on around their place."

"Let us pray," said Paul.

Kneeling they each offered a prayer for Omne and for help to find him.

Paul closed the little prayer session. "Our Father, we come to you today requesting your help. Our friend, Omne, is missing. Only you know where he is. If he is in trouble we ask for your advice. Show us where he is and may we find him in time. Then, Father, show me how to help him. He is a very troubled man but I am sure he is searching for help. Now I thank you for answering our prayers. I ask this in the name of our LORD, Jesus who died for us and is now with you. Amen.

Tychicus, you go look around. Try to listen to what folk are saying. Ask questions without sounding too snoopy. Better go down near the arena as he might have walked that way and there are always men standing around down there. You will not look like a stranger but still be very careful."

"Shall I take Simon and Thomas? They might be a help to me."

"No, Simon and Thomas should stay here. It would look suspicious if all of you went and the men there might remember Simon and Thomas as being with Omne earlier."

Tychicus started out, stopping at several small fruit stalls, always keeping his eyes and ears open. He continued his way. This was not a good part of town and he did not like to be here even in the daylight. Men still slept off their stupor as they lay sprawled on the roads or steps of the buildings.

Everything blared danger, walk carefully and keep alert.

"Oh God, my Father," he prayed silently, "Please send your angels to help me and to guide me. Protect your servant from all harm and watch over Omne. He needs you and I think he wants you." Thus Tychicus searched and prayed as he went.

Then he heard a voice speaking above the others. "Sure I did," the man growled. "He never had but a few small coins on him. He was a waste of time."

Another man now spoke up. "What did you do with him?"

"Oh I let him fall asleep and then after I took his few coins I was so angry I beat him. I left him chained to a post in the shack."

"Is he alive?"

"I don't know. But with the beating I gave him and no one to help him I don't think he will live for long. In a few days we can throw his body into the river. Too many of his kind here anyway."

"That is for sure. He sure could not drink much wine," laughed another. "After only 2 or 3 glasses he was in a stupor."

Tychicus waited quietly as he listened, trying to hear everything the men said but the men were walking down the road and their voices faded away. "It must be Omne who the men were talking about but where is he? How can I find him in time?"

Looking carefully towards the men Tychicus saw that they were standing in the street near a small eating place.

Though it was not the cleanest place, Tychicus decided to stop and order some food to eat. That way he would not look like he was snooping as he waited to hear more. He took a spot nearest to where the men were. They were not far away now and were still talking loudly.

"Maybe the rats will eat his body. We will not have to worry about him that way. Was he where he might get wet in high water?"

"Yes. I thought the river might rise last night and if it had, he would have drowned."

"So he is near the river", Tychicus whispered to himself. "Well I am getting closer. But still I can't look along the complete length of this river. I will just have to wait a little longer."

"Well that old house is ready to fall down anyway. Maybe we ought to help it out. We could light a fire there tonight. It is far enough from the other houses so they will not burn."

"That is a good idea. Tonight when it is the darkest. We will all meet there. Okay?"

"Hey, wait a moment," spoke another man. "I don't know where to go."

"That is right. You have never been there. You go to the mud dam near the Blue Ghost night house. Turn left and follow that road to the large sycamore tree, you know, that huge tree. It is right behind the tree next to the water."

"Oh I know where that is. I will be there."

Tychicus left the shop and returned to Paul's house. He rushed in and told the news. I am sure that is where Omne is. He needs our help now. I think Simon and Thomas should help me!"

"Yes," said Paul. Go now but be very careful. Do not go back through the area where you just came from. Go around that place."

CHAPTER 10

"We must be careful," Said Tychicus as the three men left Paul's house. "Walk fast but still try not to attract any attention to us. Just walk like we are going to market! I hope Omne is still alive; it sounded like he was beat up quite severely! Keep an eye open for anything unusual but do not stare at anything or anybody! The house may be guarded so when we find it we must approach with extreme caution!"

They skirted the main part of the city and finally came to where they believed they would find Omne.

"There is the Blue Ghost Night House," said Thomas. "Is that the large tree they talked about?"

"Yes, I do think so. I wonder if he is in that little shack over there by the water's edge.

It looks like it is about ready to fall down. I don't think anyone lives here anymore but we had better approach slowly. It sure is a filthy place."

The three men walked up to the shack and knocked on the barred door. There was no answer from inside so the men walked around the shack to see if there was another way in.

"Look here," said Tychicus. "Here is a low window that I think we can crawl through if we can get to it. The water is almost lapping at the lower wall; be careful that you don't slide into the water. It looks quite deep here." He crept carefully along the muddy ridge to the window. "I can't see anything inside so we will have to go in. At least we will not be easily seen over here." And with that he crawled into the dark, rotten building. Simon followed him, the weather worn wall swaying slightly as he slithered through.

Thomas stood guard and kept watch as Simon disappeared inside. Softly to himself Thomas prayed, "LORD, I am new at this praying business but I believe you will hear my faltering words. Please help us find Omne and may we reach him in time to save him." He shuddered as he looked at the old building.

"He is here," Tychicus whispered. "Over here in this corner. But we need a way to carry him. He is alive but he doesn't respond to me at all. We need a horse and a cart. Where can we get one?"

"Say," Thomas spoke up, "I might know someone." then looking at Simon he continued, "don't the people where we stay have a horse and buggy? I am sure they do."

"Yes," Simon answered. "They do."

"I will stay here with him. You two go for help." As the two others left, Tychicus crawled back into the shack. He untied Omne and tried to make him more comfortable. Omne's face was badly bruised and the area around his eyes was black and blue and swollen. One leg was twisted and Tychicus feared it might be broken. It was cold and very damp in the shack, and so dark he could see very little. The room stunk with the rotting garbage that lay everywhere. It was apparent that this house had been used for this same purpose before. "Well," thought Tychicus, "if they burn this shed down they can't use it like this again. It sure is a mess and full of rats too," he added as he saw a large gray form dash across the floor and disappear into a hole.

Time went so slow for Tychicus and his heart began to fear. "Oh God, you who are all Wise, who know the end from the beginning, we need you now. Help us find a way to get Omne to safety soon. Keep Thomas and Simon safe and give them success."

When the two men arrived at their room, the man of the house met them. Hurriedly they told what they needed and why.

"I will help you," the man said. "The horse is in the stable out back.

You can help me get the cart hooked up to the horse." Sometimes I think Rome must be about the most wicked city on earth. There is so much violence here anymore, not at all the way it was when I was young." "I was concerned about Omne when you said this morning that he had not come in last night. He doesn't look like someone who would seek trouble."

It was noon before they got started. Again they went in the way that would draw the least attention to themselves. It was longer, but safer. They had to wind around the outer edges of the city yet careful that they were going in the right direction.

"This road is blocked ahead," the man said. "We will have to turn down this side road."

They had just made the turn when a workman, in grimy clothes, stopped them. "Hey, where are you going?"

"We are going to get a load of rock; I am making a wall and was told I could get some good rocks down here," the man lied.

"Okay, but you will have to go to your Left at that corner."

"But that is the wrong direction? I need to go Right to get where I can get the rock!"

"You will turn Left," the man growled."

"We will turn Left," the man said.

"Why did you say we wanted to go Right? We have to go left if we are to get to the river?" Thomas said.

"I know," the man replied, but to the right is where the rocks are. If I had said I wanted to go left he might have questioned me for there are no rocks down here."

Several times they had to turn and try another route always with mounting fear that someone would question them about their activity.

Arriving at the shack they found that Tychicus had managed to unlock the door. Gently they wrapped Omne in heavy blankets and laid him in the cart. Now it looked like they had a body that they were taking to bury and as this was not uncommon they went the shortest, most direct way to where Paul was. The trip was short and soon Omne was lying on a mat in Paul's room. To avoid drawing attention to them, the man with the horse left immediately.

Turning to Tychicus Paul said, "Go see if you can find Luke. I need him now. He might be in the temple just around the corner."

"I know where. I will get him."

While Tychicus was gone, Paul and the others carefully took Omne's clothes off of him. Thomas noted that these clothes were the new ones which Omne had purchased from a local tailor only two days before. He had looked so handsome in these new clothes as they fitted his trim body well. Now they were torn and filthy with mud, vomit, blood and his own body waste. The odor was terrible as the men undressed him.

The new clothes were now nothing but garbage. He would never wear them again. Tenderly they cleansed his body, cleaning the filth away showing the many bruises and cuts. All this time Omne did not know or even feel them. The only sign of life within him was his unsteady breathing and heart beat. Otherwise he was limp and lifeless. "Dear God," prayed Paul reverently, You know this man. If he has work to do for you please raise him up again. Help us know what to do for him. We are your servants and he is also one of us. Thank you LORD." Then Paul and Thomas gently turned Omne to finish their cleaning. Satisfied that he was thoroughly clean and they could do no more they covered him with a clean covering and again Paul prayed to his Friend above.

Paul had just finished his last prayer when Tychicus and Dr. Luke entered the room. Immediately Luke took over the care of Omne.

Drawing the others aside Luke said quietly, "His condition is not good, it is very grave." Then turning to face Paul he asked, "is this the man that you told me about last night? You said he was very troubled. If that is the case I fear he may not have the will left to fight for his life. Without a fighting spirit he will not make it. His injuries are not that serious but his spirit may be broken. What do any of you know about him?"

Simon answered, "All I know is that he thinks he has been too wicked for God to love him. He is carrying a great burden. But I feel there is hope in his heart even yet as he had expressed a great desire to see and talk to Paul. It seems that one of Paul's friends was at his house long ago and he still remembers his instruction."

"I am sure he is a good man as he is so kind. I would not be here today if it wasn't for him," added Thomas.

Paul looked at Thomas then asked, "Why do you say that?"

"It is a long story but as you remember I was very hard on the slaves. On this trip I was especially mean to them and even severely injured one of them. I was forced to carry the slave's load and Omne helped me. It was because of his love and kindness that I even made it. Because of him and Simon here I am a changed man." Then slowly shaking his head he added, "No, I do not believe Omne is a bad man. Troubled, yes he is, but I am sure there is hope for him."

"Where is he from?"

"I really don't know for sure but I think he came from Colosse or near there."

"I have never been in Colosse but I remember that my friend Epaphras was there several years ago. I will search this matter. I think the LORD will raise him back to full health. We must not give up faith. His name is Omne? That is an odd name, one I have not heard before. I wonder if it is only part of his name. Turning to Dr. Luke he asked, "Is there anything you need for him?"

"I need some of that special ointment that you have, to put on his sores, but otherwise just time. You have cleansed him well. Also when we talk around him, we must always include him. No negative talk. Always talk encouragement. Assure him of your friendship and especially of God's love for him."

The men took turns caring for Omne with Paul at his side much of the time, talking soothingly to him. There was no change in Omne, yet with the good care given him, his wounds and bruises began to heal.

The next day Tychicus took a walk around to the old shed where they found Omne. "Well they did it," he told the others. "They burned the old shed down. One less shed for the rats to infest. Good thing we found Omne when we did."

One day as Thomas was sitting with him alone Omne started to talk. It was very soft and hard to understand and he still didn't open his eyes. He was obviously talking like one in a sleep. Excitedly Thomas called for Paul who was nearby and the two listened to Omne's story. It did not come all at once but Omne would whisper a few lines and then be silent for awhile.

At first the words did not make sense to the men. But as time went on they were able to put part of his story together. For the first time they heard that he was a run-away slave. They heard that he was married and often he called out for Martha or for Jerad. Martha, they supposed was his wife. But who was Jerad?

"So that is why?" Thomas said softly.

"Why? What are you talking about, Thomas?"

"Now I know why Omne took such good care of the slaves. He knew how it was to be a slave and I am sure he has been mistreated."

"You could be right," put in Paul.

There were other names too but the name of Jerad or Martha were spoken the most. Still more days went by and he remained silent. One day he fairly screamed, "where are you Jerad." Later he moaned, "Oh Martha, Martha, I miss you." One day he whispered "Philimon."

"Philimon," Paul replied. I was told about a man called Philimon. Epaphras stayed with him and his household. He became a good Christian, a kind man too. Could it be the same man?"

"I need money," Omne said one day. Still he would not respond to questions from the men.

It was five days after Omne was beaten when another man entered the house. His name was David. Paul greeted him warmly and introduced him to the other men there.

David was just there for a few weeks on a trip from far away. He was about to return to his home and stopped in to see his friend Paul. David was the older son of a farmer who lived a few days travel from Colosse. He was a strikingly handsome young man and showed his thoughtful demeanor. He had always lived at home and helped his father care for the farm. Then he became dissatisfied with his life. He wanted to see the world and despite his father's warning of the wickedness that was out there, and his mother's tearful pleas he packed his few things and went to see the world. He soon found that the world was not what he wanted and planned to return home. He had found Paul several weeks ago and promised to visit him again. Now he was back to tell Paul that he was going home soon.

"Who is that man on the mat?" David asked.

"His name is Omne. He was beaten severely and we are caring for him. We think he is from Colosse though we know little about him. But it now appears that he is a run-away slave. Yet we know he is searching for the LORD too. We are trying to help him but he still does not respond."

Paul said to David, "You know, Omne looks a lot like you. That is strange. Same eyes, hair and about the same body build."

"He does at that. But I sure do not know him. Paul, I am not going home right now after all. I feel impressed to wait around a few more weeks. There is a merchant here in town that wants me to help him and I said I would think about it.

Do you think I am doing the right thing?"

"Are you changing your mind about going back home?"

"Oh no! I want to go home. They need me there, but this will only take a few weeks longer and I will earn needed money for my family."

"You will be fine, David. Will you return to see me again before you leave. Somehow I want you to meet Omne. I can't say why, but feel impressed that you need to talk to him."

"I will return. If I can help in any way I will be glad to do so. After all that you have done for me how can I refuse."

"David, I remember you. You are the same man that was on that ship with me several months ago. Do you remember me? I was a guard for the slaves and not very kind either," Here Thomas hung his head in shame.

David looked closer at Thomas and a smile broke across his face. "I remember you, and for sure, you were most cruel. But look at you now! You look like a new man. You have found the LORD I can tell."

"Yes, thanks to Omne and Simon and now Paul, I am a changed man. Life is good again."

"Omne helped you? I thought he was troubled. Does he know the LORD too?"

"He does, but is fighting something which we still do not know what. But his life still shows his belief even when he denies it."

The morning after David left Omne opened his eyes and looked around. "Where am I? "he whispered.

"You are in my house," answered Paul.

"Why?"

"Do you remember leaving here one day and getting beat up?"

For several moments Omne lay there, his eyes large with fear as he searched the room.

"Do not fear, you are safe here. I am Paul your friend."

Finally recognition showed in Omne's eyes and at last he spoke again. "How long has it been?"

"Six days now. You were badly beaten. Do you remember it?"

"Some men blocked my path and I was taken to a dimly lit night-house where I was forced to drink strong wine. Later I was taken to another shack. That is all I remember."

"Well you are safe here." Then as Luke entered the room Paul said, "This is Dr. Luke. He has been caring for you. He is my friend too."

Dr. Luke smiled at Omne. "Good to see you awake. It has been a long time. Now I think we had better see about getting some water and food into you. I will be right back with some." He return quickly with a hot bowl of stew. Omne was so weak that he had trouble feeding himself so Luke slowly fed the stew to him. With the food came new life to Omne. His color improved and his strength increased rapidly.

Still it was several more days before he was able to sit up for very long and still longer before he was able to walk. Though he was satisfied with Omne's progress, Luke was still worried about Omne. He still would not talk about himself or his problems.

One day as Omne was sitting up Paul came to him. "Omne, we have been caring for you for a long while now. How about answering a few questions for me?"

"I will try," Omne answered.

"Okay, who is Martha and Jerad?"

"How do you know about them?" Omne asked, obviously in great distress. His eyes grew moist and he wiped them with his arm to hide the tears that threatened to spill out.

"You talked some before you woke up from your injuries. Many times you called their names."

"Don't send me back. Oh please don't. They don't want me anymore, not now after all I have done." He turned his head away from the kind man who sat beside him. "Oh, why did it happen? No, please don't send me back!"

"We won't send you back. You can stay here as long as you want. But in order for you to heal completely you need to get rid of your deep pain, pain I could see in you the first day I met you. Now you must talk. Do you think that Simon or Thomas or Tychicus or I will harm you? Do you not know that we are your friends?"

"Oh I know you are my friends, that is why I can't tell you all my evil doings. I don't want to lose you as friends. I need you now for you are the only friends I have any more."

"What kind of friends do you think we are?"

"I am sorry. Please help me."

"Fine, now start with my question."

"Martha is my wife, or was my wife. She is most wonderful and I love her so very much. Yet I hurt her too much for her to love me anymore." Turning to the others who had just entered the house his eyes filled with tears as he pleaded for their understanding.

"Go on," added Paul. "We are listening to you."

"Well when my first-born son, Jerad died I was devastated and blamed God. How could God kill my son, the strong healthy youth, my joy? It was not fair. I knew God could have spared him if he wanted to so why did he kill him? Well I grew all the more angry and was not kind to my other children or my lovely Martha. She was so good to me, tried to help me, but I would not listen to her. My master tried to help me too, he would reason with me lovingly just like a father would." Here Omne suddenly stopped, fear again showing on his face. "Yes, I was a slave."

"A slave? We already thought so. What happened next."

"Finally I could stand it no more. I determined to leave. I stole money from my master and ran away one night."

"Do you still love Martha?"

"Do I love Martha? She is the joy of my life, or I guess she used to be. I have tried to forget her but I can't. Oh yes, I do love her. But I am sure she doesn't love me anymore."

"How about your other children? Do you love them?"

"Of course!"

"Then you have only one thing to do. You must go home."

"I can't. Don't you see? They will not want me now after what I did. And the master will put me in chains or maybe even kill me."

"What was your master like?"

"He was kind. Treated all his slaves with kindness. Martha and I were like their own family. We were treated like a son and as his family would have been treated."

"How did they treat your children?"

"Just like they were their own grandchildren."

"You have no faith in this man whom you say is so kind?"

"Can't you see. I stole from him. I ran away. I destroyed his trust in me. I can no longer be worthy to be one of his subjects. I am a disgrace to him and my family," and again the sobs tore at his weakened body. The tears flowed as he remembered his love ones far away and what he had lost.

"We will talk more later. I see why you are so troubled. But I feel that God is speaking to you. God has not rejected you. You have rejected him. He is still there and waiting for you to return to him. He did not kill Jared.

Jared died because of the sin in this world. The evil one did it, not only to snuff out his young life and thus rob him of living here, but also to destroy your growing faith in God. I leave you now with this thought. Will you allow the evil one to succeed?   Will you believe in him and not God?"

When Omne was again alone, he pondered what Paul had said.   He could see that what Paul said could be right, yet he still was not ready to let go of his burden.   "Oh God, if you are still here, if you do still love me, let me know for sure.   I want to believe but how can I.   I miss Martha so much.   If you are God, please watch over her and the children.   I need your answer soon."   With that he drifted into a troubled sleep.

CHAPTER 11

All that day the battle raged within Omne. He
wanted to believe what Paul said, that God did love
him and that it would be best to return home. But
surely his master would be angry with him. Would
Martha still love him?" These thoughts waged war
and his frustration grew. Then a new fear grew,
what if Martha had already been given to another
man? This later thought came with a mighty blow.
Martha was still a slave. So were his children.
They could be sold or married at the will of the
master. Look at all I threw away. Oh Martha," he
again whispered. "I do love you so. Are you still
mine?" His doubts and fears struggled to gain the
mastery over him and for awhile it seemed to be
succeeding.

Many miles away another was in tearful prayer
with her God. "LORD, it has been so long since Omne
left. Where is he? How is he? Is he even alive?
It has been a year now and we have not heard a word
from him. I know the master will forgive him. It
is so hard on me being alone with six children.
The master's household is good to us, still it is
not easy. There is this man, Jethro, who is
showing interest in me.

Should I forget Omne, like he is already dead,
and consider what this other man is offering me? I
am sure the master would be willing for me to marry
Jethro. He is good, a strong working slave too! I

know the master trusts him! My family is divided over this. The older ones want to wait for Omne, but the little ones need a father and they are forgetting their father, even though I try to keep his memory alive. What should I do?" Here she paused to try to understand, to listen. For several moments she remained there, quietly thinking. Then a peace came over her as if someone had replied to her questions. "Well I will wait a little longer. I still love Omne and want him if you will but send him home to me."

Back in Rome Paul was again urging Omne to allow the LORD admittance into his soul. They were alone as the others were out buying some supplies. "Did I ever tell you how I was converted?" Paul asked.

"No, I thought you were a follower of his all the time. Weren't you?"

"Well I thought I was, but I wasn't. You see I was a devout believer in the traditions of the Jews. After the LORD was put to death I tried to rid the Earth of all of his followers. You see, I thought that they were leading the people astray and that the Jewish beliefs were correct. I was most sure of myself, very vigilant for the Jewish traditions. I held the coats of those who stoned Stephen."

"You threw stones at Stephen? Who is Stephen?"

"I never threw a stone at him but I might as well have done so. I held the coats of others as they threw the stones. I still remember the peaceful look on Stephen's face as he prayed for those throwing the stones, 'LORD, do not hold this sin against them.' You see, Stephen was a great leader for the cause of Christ and the Jewish leaders hated him. I was so sure that he was wrong that I consented to his death."

"I traveled over the country hauling innocent people to prison and testifying against them so that many were put to death. Now don't look so shocked. I was most cruel in my endeavor to serve God. I didn't care if they were women, men or children. If they worshipped this Christ they had to be killed. I was convinced this movement had to be stopped.

I was headed for Damascus where I was going to gather up more Christians to take to prison, when I was stopped in my tracks. We were nearing Damascus, we, I mean myself and several guards and soldiers traveling together. Just outside Damascus I was struck by a blinding light. It was so bright and powerful that I fell to the ground. I heard a voice saying, 'Saul, Saul! Why are you persecuting me?'

'Who are you, Lord?' I asked."

"The voice answered, 'I am Jesus, whom you are persecuting. Get up now and go into the city. Someone there will tell you what you must do.'

Now the others with me heard the voice but did not see anyone. (Acts 9: 3 - 7 NCV) When I stood up I found I was blind. I could not even tell the light of the sun overhead. To me it was black. When those with me saw me stand up they got to their feet also. My companions then led me by the hand into Damascus and found me a place to stay. I was there 3 days with neither food or drink. I prayed continuously in my agony. I was fearful for my life, confused as to what had happened to me. The Jewish belief would condemn me now as blindness was thought to be the result of one's own sin.

On the 3rd day a follower of Jesus came to me. He was one of those I was coming to take to prison. He had to have a lot of faith in his LORD to come to me. You see, the night before God spoke to him in a vision and told him where he was to find me. Well Annanias came to me and said, 'Brother Saul, the LORD has sent me to you.'"

"Why did he call you Saul?"

"My name was Saul. Then, later, the LORD changed it to Paul."

"Oh I see. I never knew that."

"Well Annanias told me all the good news, how Jesus really was the Son of God. It was so plain to me now and I asked what I should do. 'Do you believe that Jesus is the Son of God?'

'Yes, I do now,' I answered. He then anointed me with oil and immediately something like scales fell off my eyes and I could again see. Then we went to the river and he baptized me in the water."

"I never knew all that had happened to you."

"Yes, you see, I too am a sinner. Now consider which is the worse; what you did or what I did?"

"Well I never killed anyone or agreed with another person who was killing people; I never took innocent people from their homes and thrust them in prison. I guess what you did."

"Yes I think that is correct. Will you still resist his pleadings? Do you believe I am a messenger of the LORD?"

"OF course you are the LORD's messenger. You could not do what you do if God wasn't with you."

"Was I a great sinner?"

"It does look like that is correct though I would never have believed it if anyone else had told me this news."

"With this news you can be assured that there is hope for you if you only will let him back in your heart."

"Paul, do you really think there is hope for me? Maybe God is tired of my actions now and won't forgive me." Doubt still struggled to keep its strong hold on Omne "Do you believe that he is God?"

"Yes."

"Did he not save me?"

"Yes he did. You are a great apostle for him."

"Are you sorry for what you did?"

"Oh yes."

"Do you want forgiveness? Will you do whatever he asks you to do?"

"Yes I want forgiveness. I am so tired of running and I miss Martha and the children so much. But will I dare go home?"

"I think God will give you the answer soon. Right now you are still too weak to travel that far."

"Paul, I have been thinking that maybe Martha isn't even mine any longer. Maybe she has been given to another man."

"I will pray for you concerning this problem. God will guide you."

"Thank you, Paul. I feel better now than I have for a long while. Maybe God does still love me. Whatever the master sets as my punishment, I will accept as long as my wife and children want me home again." He sat down and closed his eyes as he silently prayed. "Oh my Lord, please forgive me, I have been so wrong. I closed you out of my heart; I did many evil things to chase you away, to prove I did not need you but you would not leave me alone. Thank you for sending me to Paul. Give me the strength to return home. LORD, if you can forgive me, could you give my master an understanding heart and mercy towards me. I also pray that Martha will still want me. But LORD, I can't do it alone for I am weak and afraid. I ask of you strength to make the return journey and to face whatever you have for me. Thank You for not giving up on me and for Your loving help." With this simple prayer a peaceful expression replaced the former look of anxiety on his face.

Over in the corner, another man was praying for this struggling soul, pleading to his Friend above for wisdom in guiding this babe in Christ and for giving this man his wife and family back. "LORD, if I have found grace in your eyes I plead for your leading in this man's life. Now I thank you for answering my prayer according to your great love and wisdom."

Just then Simon and Thomas entered the room. One look at Omne and they could see the difference. His face was more relaxed, the worry lines of yesterday were already fading. His eyes shone brighter than they had seen them before.

"Omne," Simon said, "You look different. What has happened?"

"I found the LORD! He does love me!"

"Wonderful," was all the others could say.

With his new hope and faith, Omne found a strong desire to live and he worked harder to regain his physical strength and mental ability. Day by day his condition improved. There was a reason to live. He had to get well and he had to hurry at it. Too much time had already been wasted.

Daily he listened to more truths as Paul talked about his LORD. Hope grew in his heart and day by day he grew more anxious to go home. The days were brighter, the flowers more glorious, the birds singing in the trees were more pleasing to hear, and life in general was a joy.

Finally the day came when Omne was able to take a walk in the city with Tychicus. Simon and Thomas had already left, having rejoined their former pack train master. They had both promised to hold fast to the truth and to come see Omne in Colosse one day.

Now as he walked about the city with Tychicus he was looking forward to the day when he too, would go home.

Suddenly Omne stopped. Turning to his friend Omne whispered, "Tychicus, we have to go back."

Tychicus looked at his friend. Omne's face had blanched and the old fear shone in his eyes. "What is it Omne," he asked as the two men turned back towards Paul's place.

"The men, I saw the men that tried to kill me. I saw the men who had stopped me and led me into the house. There was also the man who I thought was a friend, the one who must have beaten me. Oh I wonder if they recognized me."

"I doubt if they knew you. You have changed much since that day. But it is good that we did not go any closer to them.

Omne was afraid to walk in the city after that. He and Tychicus would walk in other directions and were always on the lookout for the cruel men but they never saw them again. Omne's fear for his life did not stay with him long. The LORD's peace filled him and again the look of serenity covered his face.

One day after returning from a long walk, Omne laid down on his mat. It was quiet in the house and he thought he would take a short rest. His body was healing fine and his face bore the look of one who is at peace with his God. Tychicus was sitting near the window reading, when he heard someone at the door. Opening the door Tychicus exclaimed, "Welcome back David! It is good to see you. Please come in."

David looked over at Omne resting on his mat and a surprised look flashed across his face. "Well you sure do look better. Are you really the same man? Your whole countenance shines, just like one who has found the LORD and who can now trust in him. Could this be right?"

"Yes I am doing much better thanks to the good care given to me. And it is true, the LORD has finally gotten through to me; His love has won at last. Now I must soon return to my family and submit to the LORD'S leading." But do I know you? Were you here before?"

"I was here right after you were injured. You were still sleeping and no one knew yet if you would live or die. You sure did look a mess, bruises and cuts all over your body! To me you looked like you would never survive. I guess I did not have the faith that Paul & Tychicus here had."

The men visited late into the night. Paul & Tychicus told about Omne's conversion and asked what news David brought.

"Are you going home soon now?" ask Paul.

"Yes, I am planning on going home just as soon as I can get ready. I am anxious to see my family now?" David replied.

Omne watched the men as they talked, and joy filled his heart! These were his friends!

Later, while lying on his sleeping mat, Omne could not sleep. Something David had said had awakened new thoughts in his mind. He thought of their likeness to each other. David had said something about his parents that had Omne thinking. He could not place just what it was but something had sounded familiar to him. Wild thoughts flowed through his mind thus stopping any chance of sleep coming. It was with extreme effort that Omne finally relaxed and fell to sleep.

In the morning Omne asked David if he would tell him about his family.

"I have 2 other brothers and 3 sisters. I am the oldest. We live with our parents on a ranch just out of a small village. The nearest town of any size is Colosse which is about 3 days hard travel away."

"You are the oldest child."

"Yes I am. There used to be another brother. He was 2 years older than I. But he disappeared one day and we never heard from him again." Looking at Omne he saw the look of hope and yet the look of fear in his eyes. "Omne, what is it? Are you okay?"

"Yes, I am fine! Do you remember the older boy's name and how long ago did this happen?"

"It was when I was almost 13 years old. His name was Onesimus."

"That is my name. I was taken away from my home by a group of slavers. My parents and younger brothers and sisters were gone and I was alone plowing in the field with my team of oxen."

"That is just what happened to my brother. He was gone when we got home. Father looked all over. We saw the tracks in the dirt near the oxen and were sure that he had been stolen away. I wondered why the oxen were not taken. My father said that the great beasts would have been too slow; he said the men had to hurry. We asked everyone we could but never heard from my brother again. I remember my mother crying over the loss of her eldest son. I would try to comfort her even though I was hurting too. I missed him so much. But I had little time to worry as now I had to help father in the fields. It was hard work and father tried to make it easier for me, yet they were long days and my childhood time was over. I remember I would get so tired and at night I would cry myself to sleep.

If anyone else knew I cried at night, they did not
let it be known.   I often wondered what he was
doing or where he was, but as the years went by I
thought of him less.   I guess the loss of him was a
part of the reason I left home to see the world.   I
had to work so hard from such a young age and it
all finally caught up with me."

Here he paused as he thought of home.   "Well I
will be going home soon now.   I think it is time
for me to marry too.   I hope she is waiting for
me."

"Your father's name is Jared?"

"Yes!" David answered, shock showing on his
face. "How do you know his name?   I have told no
one my father's name!"

"Well I think I am your brother!"

"What? My brother? How can it be?" David sat
there on the stool and stared at Omne.   His face
showed his shock. "After all these years can it
really be you?"

"I think I am.   My full name is Onesimus.   I
started going by Omne after I was taken away."

"Onesimus, Are you really my brother?   But you
do look like me.   One more question please.   What
are the names of my two brothers."

"The one just younger than you is Enos and the
baby was named Bethuel, and your sisters are named
Sarah, Ruth and Rebecca."

Jumping up and running over to Omne, David
grabbed him and said, "Indeed you must be my long
lost brother.   Oh praise the LORD in Heaven.   He
has brought us together at last."

Tearfully the two brothers shared news of family
and their life.

"I named my eldest son Jared after my father,
but he died sometime before I left home.   My second
son is named David, after you."

David told of their family.   "Both of our
parents are still alive and in good health.

One sister and a brother are married and live
near by.   The farm is very productive and our
family continues to grow as grandchildren are

added.   There had been no more raiders in the land
and folks living there are no longer fearful of
their children being stolen away.   The land enjoys
peace.   There were two years when there was a
severe drought.   It was feared that all plants and
animals alike would die.   It was hard and our food
supply was very meager.   Yet we never went hungry
like some folk did.   It was a great relief when the
rains came and the land again grew green."

"Tell me," he added, "about you.   What happened
to you?"

"I was attacked by a group of 5 men.   I knew I
could not fight that many and I could never flee
from them so I went with them.   It was very hard
and some of the men were mean to me.   But there was
a young man, also a slave who was about my age,
with the group.   This lad was kind to me and we
became friends.   After several hard, grueling days
we arrived at a camp where I was kept for many
days.   Amil and I became close friends.   We were
each others only friend and depended on each other
for support.   It was a sad day when I was taken
away.   Amil, had told me about his God and
encouraged me to worship and trust him.

I was sold to a rich man.   This man was very
kind.   He gave me a wife, the most lovely girl I
have ever seen.   Martha and I were so happy.   This
man was of the Jewish belief.

One day a stranger came by and taught my master
about Jesus.   My master later helped Martha and I
believe.   We were so happy, treated like their own
family.   Happy, that is, until Jared died.   Then I
just fell apart.   I rejected God, stole from my
master and fled.   Thanks to good friends and more
praise to God, I have at last come to my senses.   I
am going home just as soon as I am well."

"I am so glad to hear that.   Father and Mother
also believe as we do.   I too am anxious to get
home."

"They no longer worship that ugly silver image?
I used to think he was so ugly and I was scared of
him.   But mother said I was not to talk against the

god for fear of his doing bad things to us. For a long time I thought it was this god that had caused me to be kidnapped."

At this David laughed, "Hey, that sounds just like me. I was so frightened of the god. He was really ugly, wasn't he? But he is no more. Several years ago he was melted down into silver bars and coins."

Omne spent many hours seeking help from God.

One day he was talking to Luke. "Say Luke, when can I go home?"

"Well it is true that you are doing great now. You are gaining your strength and your wounds are almost all healed. Still I feel it would be best if you waited at least another two weeks. I think you will be ready to travel at that time."

"Not before then?"

"I think you had better wait. I am afraid you would find the long journey too strenuous and your body might give out under the stress. I know how anxious you are to be home but two weeks will not be long," and Luke smiled reassuringly at Omne.

"David, will you wait for me?"

Looking at his newly found brother David felt the cords of love binding them together. Here was the one he had not seen for many years, the one he feared was lost forever. Slowly, with deep emotion, he answered him. "I am so anxious to get home now; I have been away far too long and it is time I returned to carry my load of work at home. You know that our parents are not the youngest anymore. I don't want to wait that long. I need to get on my way. I am planning on going tomorrow."

"That soon?" whispered Omne.

"Yes, I would like to travel with you," and here his voice broke as his mixed emotions nearly overwhelmed him. Regaining his composure he continued, "I feel I can't wait 2 weeks more. But I tell you what. Write a letter to Martha and I will see it gets to her. It is only 2, maybe 3 days travel from home and I can meet her and your family. I will then go home and tell our family that you are well and will come see them as soon as you can. Otherwise we will come to see you."

David left the next morning and Omne felt all alone. He missed David, even if they had only known each other a few days. He could feel the bond growing between them. He also looked forward to seeing his parents, brothers and sisters again. He missed his good friends Simon and Thomas. How he wanted to go home. "Oh LORD, help these two weeks to go by fast. Be with my friends and my family. Be especially close to Martha and the children. Speak to my master in my behalf too.

He paused as his thought centered on Martha. "Martha, my lovely Martha; you are the one I have loved so deeply yet hurt so much. Please wait for me!" Again tears welled up in his eyes as he thought of Martha, his parents and his home. "Father, I sure do need you now!"

CHAPTER 12

One day the master came to Martha as she was
cleaning in his house. "Martha, have you given
thought to the offer made to you the other day?
Jethro is a good man. I would not allow anyone to
even think of marrying you if I did not fully trust
him. Martha looked troubled as she turned to face
her master. "I am not ready to give him an answer
yet. I find I still think of Omne too much. I
still pray he will return and I must be waiting for
him." She studied her master's face as she spoke.
This man was more like a father than a master and
had always shown her much love. Hesitantly she
continued, "Do you think I am doing wrong? I know
Jethro will care for me and my children. But
somehow I feel I have to wait a little longer."

"Good," the master replied. "I too will
continue to wait. No, you are not doing wrong.
God will lead you! I miss him too as he was like a
son to me." Then smiling at the still lovely woman
standing before him he added, "I too think he will
return soon!

Martha sang softly as she hurried to finish her
work. It was a song that Omne had loved to hear
her sing. She did not hear her mistress enter the
room.

"Martha. You look so lovely today. I think you
are finally getting over your great sorrow. I sure
enjoy listening to you sing as you work. Is there

a reason?" She searched the younger woman's face for the answer.

"I am happy today. I don't really know why but I just feel like something wonderful is about to happen. Does that sound crazy to you?"

"Not at all. Besides whatever gives you that glow and makes you sing like the birds is most welcome to me." She smiled as she studied her maid. "You have been a blessing to me and my family for many years now. I don't know what I would do without you for I depend on you so much. You are like a daughter to me, a daughter I was never given," and she smiled warmly at Martha.

The next few days went by in a hurry.

Then one afternoon while Martha was preparing the evening meal, David rushed in. Mother, there is a man here to see you. He looks just like Father and I ran to greet him but he is not father. Hurry," and the boy ran outside.

Martha's heart beat wildly when she saw the stranger! But when he spoke she knew he was not Omne and again the great sadness filled her heart. She lowered her head and wiped away the stray tears that slid out of her eyes as she struggled to overcome her grief. Finally she lifted her eyes and looked up at the man standing before her.

"Greetings to you and your family. I bring you good news. I am David, your husband's next youngest brother." Watching Martha with keen eyes he saw her hand fly to her mouth to muffle a cry. Then as he watched she started to fall. Quickly he was at her side and gently sat her on the ground. Pausing he asked, "Are you okay? I do not want to alarm you but I really have good news for you."

Taking a few deep breaths Martha finally sat still. "I am alright now. So you are David. I knew Omne had a brother with that name but never thought I would see him. How do you know me?"

"I just came from Rome and have a message here for you. Here, read it while I wait."

Holding the letter in trembling hands, Martha read the short message. "Dear Martha, please forgive me for hurting you so. I am alive and will come to you as soon as I can travel. I miss you so much.

Martha, God is alive. My brother David will tell you the rest. Love, Omne"

Martha seemed unable to comprehend the message. Looking up at David she asked, "Is he really alive? If it is he, why did he not come home with you?"

"Omne is alive. He is doing better now."

"What do you mean by saying he is better now? Where is he? What happened to him?"

"He is in Rome. He was robbed and badly beaten, nearly killed. His doctor, a friend of the Apostle Paul, said he could travel in another two weeks. I would say that he will be leaving Rome any day now, if he has not already left."

Suddenly, regaining her composure, Martha jumped up and exclaimed, "Oh the food, I need to get the meal finished." Then as David started to leave she added, "Please stay and eat with us. I could never allow you to leave here at night. It is not safe. You can leave in the morning."

By now all the children were gathered near Uncle David. They ran wild with excitement at the news. They were so happy that their father was coming home.

That night passed as in a whirlwind. Martha kept David talking most of the night.

Martha arose after only a few hours sleep, to fix the morning meal and to prepare Uncle David a good lunch to take with him. She would have to hurry if she was to get to her mistresses place on time. But her whole being was filled with such excitement that hurrying was impossible.

When she walked into her mistresses house her face was still flushed.

"You look like something exciting or terrible has just happened," her mistress said.

"I woke up late and had to hurry". Martha could not tell her good news at this time. Later she would tell but for now she hugged the wonderful news to herself. As she started at her work she hummed a tune quietly. Oh the sheer joy that filled her whole being. Her Omne was really alive and coming home.

The older woman was still concerned for her maid and thought maybe she should give her the day off from work. The past year had not been easy for Martha.

"Martha, would you like the day off?"

Horrified, Martha looked at her. She would not know what to do with a whole day off. "Am I doing poorly at my work?" she asked.

"Your work is excellent like it always has been. I just thought you might like one day off."

"No, I am fine." Then to prove it she returned to her work with a vengeance.

Still the older woman was not satisfied. "Maybe I had better check with Seth and see if he knows what is wrong with Martha." Seth was most concerned when he was given the message that his mother wanted to see him right away. His mother seldom called for him and he was afraid that she was ill or in some distress. "Amon," he called to one of the slaves nearby, "take over here. I have to see what mother wants and will come back as soon as I can. You know what to do.

"Mother, what is it? Are you sick?"

"I am fine, my son. But I am worried about Martha.

She came to work this morning a little late and if I am not wrong, I'd say that something serious has happened to her. From her actions and response I think it was good news but she has not told me what it is. Do you think you can find out for me? I am worried about her."

"I will look right into the matter," Seth answered as he smiled with relief that his mother was well. "I will go now. I wonder if the news Jethro told me might be true?"

"What did he say?" asked his mother, concern showing on her face.

"He had seen a man enter Martha's house last evening and it appeared he stayed there all night."

122

"Oh! Who?" his mother asked.

"No one seems to know; he was a stranger. But it appears that the children welcomed him too! Now don't worry," he said to his mother, "I am sure it is all fine. I will find out for you."

Later in the day Seth came to where Martha was cleaning. "Martha, is it true? Oh tell me it is."

Teasingly Martha answered, "Is what true? What are you talking about?"

"Now don't you tease me. You know what I am talking about. I have to know if what I have heard is true. Oh, please tell me it is true. Is Omne coming home?"

She need not have answered for her shining eyes and lovely smile spoke for her.

"Then it is true. Oh praise our God. Does father know yet?"

"Not unless he has heard from the same source you did. I was planning on telling him and your mother this evening but I now know that I had better tell them right away."

Meanwhile Omne too was excited. He was finally on his way. He was thankful he was not traveling alone. Tychicus was accompanying him. Tychicus also had a letter from Paul to give to Omne's master in behalf of Omne. They were to travel back the way he had come; to Troas and on to the village where Amil lived. As anxious as Omne was to get home he had to share his news with Amil even if it made his trip many days longer and thus delay his homecoming. But Amil was such a good friend and Omne knew he owed much to him.

"Omne," I am sure I know a shorter and better way to get from your friends place to your home. I believe I have been over that very road before. We will check it out with Amil," Tychicus said.

Omne was glad for the letter that Paul had written. Though he was sure his master would forgive him, he was still fearful. Paul's letter brought much encouragement to him. He knew most of the contents of the letter as Paul had read it to him.

The journey to the coast was not difficult for which the travelers were thankful. Even so, Omne soon realized the wisdom of his not being allowed to leave sooner. He grew very tired and had to rest often the first day but day by day his strength improved. Still it was nearly three weeks before they reached the port city where they were to board the ship.

The voyage to Troas was very rough. A storm arose and the ship tossed and rolled in the large waves. The waves crashed against the little ship as it tried to make its way. The storm lasted for 2 days and all on board grew weary. It was with great joy and relief when on the 3rd day the storm blew itself out and the sun rose bright and warm overhead. With joy the crew discovered that they were still on coarse. On the tenth day they spotted the harbor near Troas.

Tychicus and Omne stayed in Troas for 2 days, visiting with some of Paul's friends before going on their way.

It was a different Omne who early one afternoon knocked at the door. When Amil opened the door his expression was of shock. Then he threw open the door and grabbed Omne in a large hug. "You look grand. You have found the LORD again I can tell by your face."

Omne answered his friend. "Yes I found the LORD and I am going home at last. Amil, This is my friend Tychicus. He is also a friend of Paul's. But what is wrong? You don't look so good. What is the matter?"

"Come in," Amil said softly as he stepped out of the doorway. His shoulders drooped like one carrying a heavy load. "You must be tired." Then as the two travelers entered the house Amil said, "I have to be going out now," and his voice broke. Daniel is missing."

"Daniel," whispered Omne. In his mind he could see the little boy, rudy and strong, a picture of perfect health playing in the yard in front of the house. "Gone?" he asked. "What do you mean, 'gone'? Why when I was hear that little boy was my constant shadow." Again he asked, "what do you mean he is gone?" Omne could see terror in Amil's eyes as he looked at his friend.

"I have to go," and Amil was gone without answering the question.

Omne turned to look at Amil's wife who was standing by the open door, tears streaming down her cheeks. "Can you tell me what has happened to the boy?"

Struggling to regain her composure the woman at last answered. Yesterday afternoon Daniel went out to play like he does all the time. But later when we called to him there was no answer. Amil, his parents and many others have been searching ever since and still have not found him. I am afraid he is gone forever," and again the tears ran unchecked down her face.

Omne turned to see Tychicus motioning for him to come outside. Walking out to where his friend was already kneeling on the dirt Omne went to him and knelt also. Both men prayed fervently for the lost boy, for his family and friends who were searching. Omne ended his prayer with, "LORD, not this boy too. If he is still alive help us find him. Show me what to do, Thy will be done."

Standing, up Omne started down the trail that led to the small river. He knew that the lad liked to play here but surely many had already searched here. Still he felt drawn to the water. Reaching the gentle flowing stream he stopped to listen. The only sound was the gurgling of the water and the breeze in the trees, even the many birds were silent. Occasionally he heard someone calling for Daniel but they seemed far away.

He continued searching as he walked up the streams bank. There was little brush and only a few small trees growing near the stream with no great hiding places where the boy could be.

Again he prayed for help and he felt like a hand was leading him up the stream's edge farther away from the small town.

At last he stopped. "It is no use going any farther," he thought. "I had better go back and look somewhere else." Then he heard a soft whimper. Quickly Omne turn around and started toward a shallow hole he could see in the bank. Drawing closer he spotted a small foot sticking out. "Daniel," he shouted as he rushed to the spot. "Daniel, what happened?"

The boy showed pain and fear as Omne drew near. Then recognition shown on the boys face and he said, "Uncle Omne, how did you get here. I want to go home."

Kneeling by the boy's side Omne noted that one of the boys legs was caught between two large rocks that lay at the mouth of the cave. Somehow the boy's foot had slipped in the crack between the rocks and had lodged there, pinning the boy fast.

Carefully Omne worked to free the lad. Joy and thanksgiving filled him as he clawed away at the rocks that held the small boy secured. Still the boy's leg remained stuck fast.

Looking around him, Omne saw a piece of a tree limb. He went over and picked it up. Returning to the boy he pushed the limb between the rocks, near Daniel's leg. "Son, I am going to see if I can pry these rocks apart with this stick. I want you to pull as I try to spread these rocks apart.

Putting pressure on the limb, Omne prayed it would not break. Then, ever so slightly, he felt one rock move a little. In a flash the boy had his leg out. Gathering him up into his strong arms Omne headed back to the boy's home.

"Oh Daniel," shouted his mother as she saw Omne carrying him up the trail. "Oh Daniel, I was so afraid you were gone forever."

Laying the boy on his sleeping mat Omne went in search of Amil.

That evening after all the searchers had returned and heard the good news the three men sat resting on the front step.

"I still don't understand how you found him," Amil said."

"It was like I was being led there by an unseen force," replied Omne. "Will he be okay?"

"The doctor said that all he needs is rest, food and a couple days off that leg and he will be fine."

"Praise the LORD," said Tychicus. "The LORD still lives."

Turning to Omne Amil asked, "Now will you tell me all that has happened to you since you left here. The change in you is startling.

I am also so grateful that you came at just the right time; you saved our son." Amil's eyes were moist as he looked at his friend while he plied Omne with questions. It was with difficulty that Amil's wife was able to serve them food.

That evening Amil's parents came over and the talk continued until late in the night.

The next day the friends continued their conversation as they walked around the small town. "I am so thankful that our LORD was with you and that you finally let Him back in your heart," Amil said more than once. "You are a different man than the one who left here."

Though he was pressed to stay another day, Omne would not tarry any longer. "I am so anxious to see Martha. I have already been gone too long and I have to hurry home."

The next morning, as he was getting ready to leave, he felt a small hand grasp his larger one. Looking down he saw Daniel's large, brown eyes staring soberly up at him. "Uncle Omne, do you really have to leave now?"

Taking the small boy in his arms Omne said, "Yes, I need to go. I need to see my little boys and girls that I left behind."

"I am sure glad you came when you did for you found me. I was so afraid! Thank you Uncle Omne." There were tears in the little boys eyes as Omne sat him back on the floor.

"Tychicus," said Amil, "the road you talked about is the best one. You will need to sleep one night on the way. But the night will not be cold and you will be safe this way as it is well traveled. There is a spot for travelers to stay and you will reach it just before sundown. It will only take you another 4 hours the next day to reach Colosse. Good by my friends and may God go with you."

Omne looked at Amil. "You say it will take us less then two days to get home. It took me many more days to get here when I left; it must be a lot shorter."

"Oh it is not far this way, my friend. You went the long, hard way around to get here and are going back by a nearly straight route. It will not be difficult."

Omne was so anxious to get home yet still fearful of his arrival. How would his family and his master react to his coming home?

CHAPTER 13

It was a beautiful morning as the men started on the last part of Omne's long journey. True to their information, the road was an easy one. One could tell that many people traveled on this road for it was well worn with wagon wheel tracks showing plainly in the now dusty road. The road was not busy and the two enjoyed the quietness of the countryside. The road wound gradually uphill, dropping down at times to cross a little stream then climbing back up, trying to make up for the lost elevation. It wound ever so gently around rock bluffs, passed several large caves, occasionally through dark gorges and narrow ravines. At these places Omne was glad he was not alone for the vision of the bandits was still real to him. But besides Tychicus's company he felt the presence of his God, whose presence was not felt on his earlier journey. That journey had been cold and frightful. Now it was warm and friendly.

Omne was now restored to full health. No longer did Tychicus have to wait for him to rest. His face and whole body showed his vigor, his health.

Except for an occasional fear relating to his home-coming, his face still glowed with his anticipation of that reunion. His whole body tingled with the desire to see his wife and family.

They found the rest area for the night. There were several others there too, but they found a

secluded spot and prepared for the night.   Nearby
was a spring, its water bubbling joyously forth out
of the rocks to start its long descent to the
valley floor.   Its cold, refreshing goodness was
reviving to the tired travelers.

From their camp they watched a pair of eagles as
they soared high above them on wings which seemed
never to move.   Far below them they saw a clearing
with miniature buildings in it.   They could see
sheep, which looked like tiny specks of white
cotton on the green fields.   They watched as the
sun dropped over the Western horizon, turning the
sky to beautiful colors of pink, reds and
lavenders.   Watching the beauty of the sunset
Tychicus said, "Isn't God wonderful to make all
this beauty just for us?"

Omne slept well that night.   He had no fear for
his life, no worry that harm would come his way.
His last words and thoughts, as he drifted off to
sleep, were, "Thank you LORD for allowing me to
return home.   Please go before me and may mercy
greet me when I arrive home.   Give me the strength
to cope with what ever is my punishment.   You are
so wonderful to me."   He slept soundly until the
early morning light spread across the Eastern
horizon awakening the sleeping birds to sing their
cheery greetings to the travelers as they prepared
to be on their way.

Tychicus and Omne ate the last of the food that
Amil and his wife sent with them; their next meal
would be with Omne's family or master.   Whatever
Omne's punishment would be, no matter how severe it
was, he knew that they would not refuse to feed the
two travelers.

Picking up their packs they headed down the
slope to the valley below.   This descent was to be
too fast for Omne and yet too slow.   Twice he
paused to utter a quick prayer to his God for
strength to face what ever lay ahead.   Several
times he asked Tychicus, "Do you still have that
letter from Paul for my master."

"Yes, I do have that letter," Tychicus would say as he tried to reassure Omne.

Rounding a curve in the road Omne stopped and said to his friend, "Look, there are the buildings of Colosse. See how they shimmer in the morning's sun? We are still several miles away but I can see them plainly."

They would not go through Colosse, but go around it. Just a little over an hour's walk now was all that remained of his great journey. The road was now level and the walking was easy. Many travelers were now on the road, most going into the city.

A few early travelers were already on their way home with their packs full of their purchases. A few of them had donkeys to carry their loads while one might even see a slow team of oxen plodding along. Omne's thoughts were at war with each other as he hurried and then slowed his pace. Fears of the unknown plagued him. "Maybe Martha no longer wants me, or worse yet maybe my master has given her to another. Or maybe my master will throw me in prison. Maybe my children have forgotten me," he would fret. Then a new fear shot throughout his body like a hot fire brand, "What if my master has sold some or all of my children to pay for my theft?" Here he trembled as he thought of this great concern.

Then he would argue, "of course Martha has waited for me and she has kept the knowledge of me alive in our children's' hearts. My master is kind, he will forgive me. Of coarse I will have to repay the money I stole from him. This will be hard to do but with God's help I can do it. My master loves my children like they are his own grandchildren. He would not sell them. I wonder if David has given Martha the letter and what her response was. Well," he said to himself, "I will soon know all the answers".

"There is the border of my master's land," he said. "In the distance you can see the dwellings of my master's family, his slaves and my family," he told Tychicus.

They were just nearing the outer fields when Omne saw a large group coming towards him. In fear he stopped and for awhile his legs nearly folded under him. Guards were coming to throw him in prison. "Tychicus, what can we do?"

"Continue on my friend. God is with you. He has led you all this way, he will not forsake you now. Do not fear the future; have faith."

The group drew closer and Omne could see many people. "Why," he said, "there is a whole army coming for me. How had they known I was coming now? See, there is my master; he is leading the group. There is Seth by his father's side and even old Simeon is coming."

He was still several hundred paces away from the group when one broke away from it and started running towards him. For a moment he stood still, then as recognition showed on his face he forgot all but the one racing to meet him. Dropping his load he raced towards the figure coming towards him. Reaching her he grabbed her and held her tightly, not knowing nor caring that the others were now near. She was still his, her face showed her love for him as she wept loudly, the months of tension flowing out of her soul. How long they stood thus, holding each other close as if fearful of losing the other if they relaxed their hold, they did not know. Then Omne felt some one tugging at his cloak. "Father, you are home. Oh how I missed you. Pick me up."

Looking down he saw one of his daughters tugging at him. He picked her up, even though she was now nearly 10 years old. "Oh Father, I missed you so. Why did you go away? Mother was right."

"What do you mean?"

"Mother kept telling us that you would return home. And you did. We prayed for you every night but you were gone so very long. Oh, I am so happy you are home. At last all will be well and we will be happy again. Now mother won't have to cry so much. Then the little girl gave her mother a hug. I know about the times you cried for father. I did too but you were right," and a lovely smile flowed like sunshine across her face.

By now all his other children were crowding around him, each trying to get his attention. All but two of them that is. The youngest daughter was standing back, a little fearful of this man whom she had almost forgotten. But when Martha urged her, she shyly came and Omne picked her up in his arms and held her close to his chest.

David stood in the background. He too was fighting an inner battle. He loved his father and was so happy to see him home yet he was angry at him for leaving them alone. It had not been easy trying to carry on when his father had run away from them. He was still standing there with down turned face when he took a quick glance towards his father. Omne was looking at him and for a moment their eyes locked on each other.

David saw the love and yes the deep regret, in his father's eyes and his heart melted within him. He could no longer with hold from his father's love. Hurrying to his father, David was unmindful of the tears that were now flowing down his face. There was only one thought on his mind as he ran to the one he had missed so long. Flinging himself into his father's arms he sobbed out, "Father, I am so glad you are home. How I missed you."

"He was the man of the house while you were gone. He carried his load like a man too. You can be proud of him," replied Martha.

"Father, I am learning how to drive a team of oxen," David said. His tears were over and a broad smile took their place.

"You are driving a team of oxen! Let me get a better look at you. You have grown a lot while I was gone; all of you have," he said, giving them all a pleased smile.

"I too missed you and am glad to be home. Your prayers brought me home at last." Then looking into David's eyes he added softly, "I am so sorry for the hardship I placed on you. I will make it up to you."

David did not answer but from the look shining on his face and sparkling in his brown eyes, Omne could feel his son's love.

Then turning to look again at Martha he added, "but you, my dear, look as young as when we were first married. You look so beautiful to me!"

Then Omne turned so he could see the large group who had come to greet him. His eyes swept slowly from one expectant face to another, resting at last on his master's sober face. Seth, still at his father's side showed his pleasure in this home coming, giving Omne a reassuring smile, but Omne could not find his answer in his master's eyes. His master's face was difficult to read. It showed neither anger or love, hurt or joy.

"I had better go see him and get it over with," thought Omne. Then he saw Tychicus walking over to his master. He watched as Tychicus handed his master the letter. Watching, Omne was shocked when his master looked at it for only a moment then put it in his garment. "Is he not even going to read it? Is he that angry at me?" Omne worried.

Now the others were greeting Omne. All were pleased he had returned. Even the one who had tried hard to fill the position Omne had left behind, seemed anxious to turn his job back over to Omne. Slowly the group was walking towards the houses. One by one the others left to return to their jobs, as they thought a great feast would be held that evening. That is it would if the master accepted Omne back. But for now they would work and hope for Omne's best. For Omne had always been a fair and just foreman. They were pleased to have Omne back and looked forward to being able to work with him again.

At last all were gone except his family, Tychicus and his master. Seth had also gone after warmly greeting Omne.

Omne pondered on Seth's parting words. He had said, "Welcome home brother. Do not fear father, but trust. I will see you later." And he was gone.

Letting go of his hold on Martha Omne walked to his master. His master's only comment was, "Come with me."

Omne went with his master, thankful that Tychicus was also coming. Somehow he felt better with his friend at his side.

Entering his master's room Omne fell on his knees. "Oh sir, I have sinned against you and against God. My sin is so great. I will be your slave for ever and try to work longer so I can repay you all. I have a little money here with me and it is yours."

Turning to Omne his master said, stand up."

As Omne stood to his feet his master said, "first I will read this letter from Paul. I will see what he has to say. All of you may sit down while I read. Taking out the letter the master began reading it. This is what the letter said.

"From Paul, a prisoner of Christ Jesus, and from Timothy, our brother.

To Philemon, our dear friend and worker with us, to Apphia, our dear sister; to Archippus, a worker with us and to the church that meets in your home:

Grace and Peace to you from God our Father and the Lord Jesus Christ.

I always thank my God when I mention you in my prayers, because I hear about the love you have for all God's holy people and the faith you have in the Lord Jesus. I pray that the faith you share may make you understand every blessing we have in Christ. I have great joy and comfort, my brother, because the love you have shown to God's people has refreshed them.

So, in Christ, I could be bold and order you to do what is right. But because I love you, I am pleading with you now instead. I Paul, an old man now and also a prisoner for Christ Jesus, am pleading with you for my child Onesumus, who became my child while I was in prison. In the past he was useless to you, but now he has become useful for both you and me.

135

I am sending him back to you, and with him I am sending my heart. I wanted to keep him with me so that in your place he might help me while I am in prison for the Good News. But I did not want to do anything without asking you first so that good you do for me will be because you want to do it, not because I forced you. Maybe Onesimus was separated from you for a short time so you could have him back forever no longer as a slave, but better than a slave, as a beloved brother. I love him very much but you will love him even more, both as a person and as a believer in the Lord.

So if you consider me your partner, welcome Onesumus as you would welcome me. If he has done anything wrong to you or if he owes you anything, charge that to me.

I Paul, am writing this with my own hand. I will pay it back and I will say nothing about what you owe me for your own life. So my brother, I ask that you do this for me in the Lord: Refresh my heart in Christ. I write this letter, knowing that you will do what I *ask you and even more.*

One more thing, prepare a room for me in which to stay, because I hope God will answer your prayers and I will be able to come to you.

Epaphras, a prisoner with me for Christ Jesus, sends greeting to you. And also Mark, Aristarchus, Semas, and Luke, workers together with me, send greetings.

The grace of our Lord Jesus Christ be with your spirit." (Philemon NCV)

It was very quiet as Philemon read the letter. He read it quietly, but still loud enough for all to hear. Omne watched his face as he read, trying to gain the answer. He sat with folded hands, a prayer in his heart, hoping fervently for God's blessing on his new life. His hands were cold and his body was shaking lightly as if he was cold. He grew most anxious as he waited. Then he heard a small voice speak quietly to him. "Be not afraid for I am with you. Be not dismayed for I am your

God. I will strengthen you, yea I will uphold you, today and forever."

Omne could feel the presence of God and he relaxed. After all, If God loved him, everything else would work out for his best. But he had to concentrate on God's promises or again he would grow fearful.

Finally, after it seemed hours since Philemon had started to read the letter, he put the letter down and looked at Omne.

CHAPTER 14

For a long moment the master was quiet. His face still wore that look of indifference. Finally, after what seemed like hours to those waiting silently, he at last looked at Omne. "Omne, tell me all that has happened to you. Why did you leave? Tell me everything. Do not leave anything out."

"Sir, it was very foolish of me to have run away. I had forgotten the God in Heaven. My story is not a pleasant one but I will tell you. You know how depressed I was over the death of Jared. I was unable to think of anything except his death. I shut out everyone else, Martha, my other children, you and even God." And so Omne told his story.

When at last he was silent Philemon spoke. "Sounds like it was only by the Grace of God that you lived to return. I can see that he has been leading you all the time.

I also know that you are not a common thief for had you been you would have taken more money from me. I wonder why you didn't take more. You knew where all of it was kept."

"Sir, I only took what I thought I would need to get me to where I could find work. And even that did not help as it was all taken from me."

"Yes I now know. Well this leaves me in a tough situation. If I take you in as before with no punishment it might lead others to do the same or even worse than you did. I have to treat you in a way so others will not do this. I am not just sure what I should do. Tychicus, will you stay here a day until I can decide Omne's fate?"

"Yes I will stay. I am headed South for a trip into Israel before I return to Paul but this can be delayed a day."

"Okay Omne. You can go to your home for today. I will call you tomorrow when I know what punishment to give you." Then as Omne turned to leave the room Philemon spoke again. "Omne, I am pleased you have returned. I can see that God has made you even better than before. I want you to know that whatever punishment I give you is not because I am angry with you."

Omne nodded his head. He well knew that the outcome would not be pleasant. Looking at his master he thought he saw a slight smile on his face.

Philemon was in great distress. He wanted to please Paul and because of his love for Omne he did not want to punish him at all. He was so glad he was home and had found the LORD. Now his service would be even better than it was before. He was positive of this. He could see his God's leading on Omne's life. Still he dared not ignore the wrong done. Oh what should he do. After much thought and prayer he called in Apphia, Seth and Tychicus. Together they would decide Omne's fate.

Meanwhile Omne was getting reacquainted with his family.

"Who was that man?" Omne asked Martha as they passed the man, while walking back to their dwelling.? I don't remember seeing him before. He sure looked unhappy."

"His name is Jethro. He is a new slave and will go free in three years. Jethro has taken a great liking for me and wanted to marry me. I was so lonely that I actually considered it before I knew you were still alive. Now how happy I am that I kept putting him off. I am so thankful that you

are home at last and that you have finally sorted
out your problems and have given your heart totally
to the LORD.   For it is only you I love, and it
will always be only you."

Omne sighed in relief as he again embraced his
wife.   "I almost lost everything that I have ever
loved," he whispered quietly more to himself than
to anyone else.

Omne had a hard time talking to Martha alone,
for the children were always with them.

Even with the uncertainty of what lay ahead for
Omne, there was peace and love in their house that
night.   There was a lot of catching up on the news,
both about his trip and the news of what happened
while he was gone.   No one voiced any fear of the
future.   Talk was centered around pleasant topics.
Omne thrilled in just being home again.

There was no feasting and no party that night.
It just could not be with Omne's fate still not
known.   Yet quietly, one by one all the other
slaves, except one, came to welcome Omne home.
Little was said, but Omne could tell their love for
him.   "I am so tired," Omne said as he sat on his
sleeping mat.   "It has been a long journey and I
feared my foolishness had caused me to lose you.
It is quiet at last with the little children
asleep. I think we should sleep too."

But just then another visitor came to the little
house.   "Omne," and Seth could not say anything
else for a moment.   Finally he through his arms
around his friend and wept tears of joy.   "Omne, I
missed you so.   I wish you had never left and I
feared you would never return.   But here you are,"
and he backed away and looked hard at the other
man. "You look good.

I can see you are a new person for you show that
you have found the LORD.   I have been in conference
with father and we have settled your fate.   I can't
tell you about it now and it bothers me much.
Still our God will be with you.   Be strong and hold
fast to your faith."

Just before the two older children were sent to their sleeping mats, David came to his father and said, "Father, can I have a talk with you?"

"Sure, my son. Let's sit out there under that old tree." Thus saying Omne put his arm around his son's shoulder and the two walked out of the house.

"Alright now, what is bothering you?"

"Father I need to ask your forgiveness. After you left I began to hate you. I would blame you for every bad thing that happened to me or to our family. For weeks I would not even mention your name or talk to anybody about you. I worked hard to help lightened mother's load but even that did not help me."

"I am sorry, my son, for the grief I caused you. I only thought of me and forgot my family."

"Father, I am sorry that I hated you but I don't hate you any more. When Jethro started showing interest in mother I started to realize just how much I still loved you and wanted you to return. Oh I am sure he is a good man but I wanted you." Here David looked into the moist eyes of his father and then suddenly burst into tears.

Sobs shook his slim body as the months of pent-up emotion were washed away.

Omne put his arms around his son and held him close until his sobbing ceased.

"I am sorry for all this pain, but I do believe I am stronger in the LORD after going through this past year. I am proud of you, David."

Finally David could again look into his father's eyes. A faint smile played across his face as he said, "Father I love you; I am so happy you came home. There is so much I want to show you and do with you," his eyes glistening.

Omne and Martha talked long into the early morning hours. "Dear, whatever lies ahead I know we can get through it. God will help us. He did not bring you home just to keep us apart. You will see."

"Yes, I know this is true but still I am concerned over the verdict. Almost any punishment will also hurt you and the children. That bothers me a lot for I have caused you too much heartache already. I can take the punishment for myself because after all it was my fault. But to see more pain put on you will nearly kill me."

"I can bare anything now that you are here. Whatever happens you will still be near. I can wait yet a little longer. I know the master will be fair."

"I know you are right but still I am worried. I love you so much. Oh why did I do such a foolish thing."

"What was done does no longer matter. You are back and I can tell that you are even a better man than before, and then you were wonderful."

"Oh how was I ever so fortunate to get you for my wife. Not only are you so lovely, you are so wise and thoughtful," and he pulled her close to him.

Omne was glad to be home again. It was so good to have Martha close to him. With these thoughts they at last fell asleep.

In the morning, all met in Philemon's office. There was Philemon, Apphia, Tychicus, Seth, Omne and Martha. Omne was relaxed as he waited for the verdict.

Finally Philemon spoke. "I do not like to do this to you, Omne. The money you stole from me was such a small amount when you could have taken much more. But this is my decision.

For 90 days you will live with the other slaves. Your work will be increased to the maximum amount that you can do. It will be most difficult and trying. The hours will be long and tiresome. During this time you will not be with Martha at all. You may speak to her when passing, but that is all. Your children can also talk to you but very little. You will be treated like all new slaves which means you will have no liberty or free time. After these 90 days I will meet with you again and tell you what next will happen. Do you understand me?"

Martha gave a gasp and her face grew very pale as she listened to Philemon give his verdict. Softly and silently the tears started rolling down her lovely face.

Omne put his arm around her and held her tight. He too paled as he heard the verdict. He looked from one to another in the room. All were sober faced and not another person in the room met his gaze.

Philemon now went on. "For today you will be able to stay with your family. Savor every moment of it as tomorrow your sentence will begin. Now you are free to go."

Philemon could not even look at Omne as he and Martha left the room. "I am sure I am doing the right thing but it seems so cruel," he whispered.

Tychicus came up to him and said, "My friend, do not fear. He will come through well and you will see that he will be better for this trial. God will help and bless him; you will see! God will also bless and guide you! Always trust in his leading. Now I must be on my way. I will stop here on my return to Rome and see how Omne is doing. May I talk to him first."

"I wish you would. Maybe you can reassure him."

Seth and Philemon stayed to converse long after the others had gone. "Father," Seth said, "I want you to know that I am with you in this decision. But may I ask one favor of you?"

"Ask, my son."

"May I give Omne a word of praise once in awhile?

It will be a hard task for him and I don't want him to become too discouraged. You know we praise even the new slaves."

"I know, my son. You may do as you want. I am glad you understand for I well know your love for Omne. I was so worried that you might not understand me, with your great joy at having him home again!" He looked at Seth long then added, "I am sure that in 90 days we will have that party that you wanted last night. I am also sure that the final results will be as you say. You may encourage him as you want. Thank you, son, for being so understanding. This is not easy for me either!"

Omne and Martha were together all that day, spending time with their children but still finding some time when they could be all alone. All others left them alone, sensing their need to be alone as a family. This day was spent to the fullest and when the next morning came, Omne left with no tears. He walked away with his head held high, not looking back at his weeping family. He walked to his new meager room and placed his few belongings in their spot. Then turning, he went out to the field and set to work.

The work was very hard. The first few nights he was so tired he could hardly sleep. As the days rolled by his aching body began to adapt to the hard work and he grew stronger. With new strength his work was also increased. Still he did not falter or complain. Often at night he would fall on his knees and pour out his heart and frustrations to his God.

But no other complaints came from his lips, no cross words fell out of his mouth, no frown creased his face. He only counted the days and planned for the day this trial would be over. What lay ahead he did not know. But his God had led him thus far and he would not forget him now.

Meanwhile Tychicus had followed a dusty, winding road; following it through low hills and fertile valleys and desert land, stopping finally at a neat, clean ranch tucked away in the hills. As he approached the buildings a young man came out. "Tychicus, you have come. Where is my brother. I told my family that I spoke to him and at first they would not believe me; now we are waiting for him to come." David was so glad to see his friend.

"Well, Omne can not come now."

David called his parents and his brothers and sisters to come meet his friend. As they all sat down to a meal, Tychicus told what had happened.

"It will be okay I am sure. Philemon, his master, is kind. No more will be given to Omne than he can bare. Still it will not be easy for Omne these next 3 months. I am sure Omne will be well treated as soon as this sentence is completed. But he will not be allowed any family to visit him and he will not be allowed any free time until these 90 days are completed. Even his children and wife can not spend time with him. All they can do is speak briefly to him when they happen to pass him."

Tychicus paused and looked around him.

David's face was a picture of deep sadness. A quick glance showed the same sadness on everyone present. "Now don't be too discouraged," he added, "somehow I have the feeling that a great reward is ahead for Omne. I can't say what for I am not sure but just from something his master's son said I think everyone will be pleased. You see, Omne saved his master's son, Seth, from drowning when he was just a lad and Seth has forever since looked up to Omne. I really feel Seth thinks of Omne more as an elder brother then one of his father's slaves! Yes, Omne will be surprised when his sentence is over!"

Brightening up, Omne's father said, "only 90 days? What is that compared to the many years he has been gone already? That will not be long. We can wait that much longer. Just to know our son is alive and well is enough for now. I thought I would never see him again. I could not believe it when David returned with the joyous news. "There were tears glistening in his eyes as he spoke these words. His encouragement brought joy to his family.

True to the instruction, Omne had no free time. His work was long, his night short. It was harvest time and everyone had to work long hours securing the harvest, but for Omne the hours were ever longer. Seldom did he even have time to speak to his family. Martha did bring him a cool drink nearly every day as he labored in the fields.

Often she brought a cool drink to all those working with Omne.

The slaves began to look forward to Martha as one watches for the cool of the evening or the coming of the refreshing rains after a long dry spell. Never did Omne speak to Philemon, though he did see him often, standing in the distance, watching him. Seth came often to encourage Omne and this did much to refresh Omne's soul.

Still as the days went by Omne did grow discouraged. He continued to do his best work but it was at night when doubts crowded his mind. "I am so tired," he would say to himself. "My punishment is great and I wonder if I will ever get through it. Why does my master only look on from a great distance? He talks to all new slaves but not to me." At times sobs shook his body as he wept in the night. Still after all of these times he would pray to his LORD and a peace would creep over his soul, calming him and allowing a peaceful sleep to follow.

But there was one who was not happy with Omne. Though he never voiced his feelings Jethro harbored dark thoughts. It was Omne's fault that his happiness was spoiled. Still he did not do anything to make Omne's work harder. Jethro would never do anything purposely to injure another person or to cause another person trouble. Still he shunned Omne and tried to keep away from him. He struggled to forget Martha for he knew she would never be his but found this to be very difficult. He would see her as she brought Omne a cool drink, see her lovely face as she smiled up at her husband, offering him encouragement.

His loss was too great and he did all he could to avoid both Omne and Martha.

Omne tried to be friendly with him but he was rebuffed. "I shall just have to try harder to be his friend," thought Omne. "He looks so unhappy." Then he smiled as he remembered why Jethro looked so unhappy. He had lost a most valuable prize. "I am sorry sir," thought Omne, "Martha is mine."

One day Jethro stumbled over a root which was at the edge of the field. He fell to the ground after first striking the plow. He lay in agony as the pain stabbed through him. Omne, who was working a short distance away saw the man fall. Stopping his team he went over and helped the man up. "Here," he said, "Lean on me. I will help you over there so you can rest. Here, let me look at your chest."

Jethro let Omne help him for his pain was great! Omne looked him over. "Looks like there are no cuts but I rather imagine you have a least one cracked rib and maybe more. You will have pain for days."

Cautiously the man stood up. He gave a short gasp as again the pain cut through him. But he returned to his work. He was after all just a slave and he would be expected to continue with his work if at all possible.

By nightfall Jethro had finished his work. He, with Omne's help, had done as much as every other day. Old Simeon, standing back in the shadows gave another sigh of appreciation. Omne was still himself, always helping others quietly.

The injured man allowed Omne to help him for two days. But he had to speak out on the third day. "Omne, why do you help me? I have had such evil thoughts about you. I have wished you were not here. Now I know you are very kind indeed. Martha was right."

"Martha?"

"Yes. I had asked the master for her. I wanted her for myself but she wanted to wait for you. Now I can understand why. Will you forgive me?"

"Of course I will," Omne replied.

And so the days went on. One day, while yoking up his oxen for the days work, one of the oxen swung his head around and his horn caught Omne in his belly. There was a pain like that Of a fire brand which shot through his whole being, a ripping sound as his flesh and clothes tore. Omne let out a loud cry and fell to the ground in pain. Other slaves working nearby gathered Omne up and carried him into his room and placed him on his mat.

CHAPTER 15

A doctor was called to stop the bleeding and to dress the wound. Carefully the doctor examined the man. "It is a nasty gash," he said at last to the expectant ones standing nearby. Still it does not appear that the horn cut any vital organs. I will try to clean the wound and sew him up. The great concern will be to stop any infection but with a gash like this I fear infection will surely come! This wound will need to be cleansed and new dressing applied every day. Can someone do that?"

"I can," spoke up Martha as she looked at her master for his permission.

"Yes," Philemon replied. "Martha will be the best to do this." He smiled at the young lady, hoping to dissolve her fears and to quiet his own fear too.

Looking at Philemon and then to Martha the doctor continued, "If no infection starts, Omne should recover completely in a few weeks. But the pain will be great until the healing is complete. I can't stress too much of the possibility of infection; if that happens," and here his voice drifted away. "Well lets just pray that no infection starts! That will be the best!"

For a week Omne stayed on or near his cot. His prayers were answered and there was no infection. But the pain was like he had never felt before, worse even than his beatings from the bandits.

At times he wanted to scream out with the pain but he bit his lips and remained silent. The only good thing is that Martha was allowed to bring him cool water and refreshing food daily. She was also allowed to cleanse his wound and redress it every day. Carefully she would wash the skin around the wound being sure to not leave any trace of sweat or grime. Tenderly she would apply the clean dressing, all the time offering soothing words of comfort. It was probably because of her good care that he recovered so quickly and remained free of any infection.

Six days after his accident Omne said to Martha, "I am going back to work in the morning."

"No, you should stay and rest longer; you might rip the wound open again. Please don't go to work yet."

"I have to," he told Martha. Every day I stay on my mat will extend my punishment longer. I want to get back with you and the children."

"We will still be there when you get through. We want you home too. But Omne, don't rush it."

"I will rest one more day, that is all," replied Omne. "I will be fine at work and not get hurt again."

After only one week he returned back to work. His stomach still hurt and often he would stifle a moan. Still he was anxious to keep working. He had to prove that he could take his punishment no matter what. Besides he had already lost 7 days. That would mean another 7 days would be added to his sentence.

At first his work was slow, but he pushed himself hard. He still had 5 weeks to go and he did not want to give a poor expression to those around him. His work had to be the best.

He was relieved to see that now he had another team of oxen. This pair was the old pair he used to work with before he ran away. It was as if the oxen still remembered him and were trying to do their best for him. They would respond to his simplest command as they plodded slowly along. As

Omne's own strength improved the oxen walked a little faster and the daily amount of work accomplished grew. Day followed day as he struggled to keep going. Slowly the pain subsided and his strength returned. He began counting off the remaining days of hard labor.

Finally the day came when his 90 days were over. "Now," he thought, "it would be over if I had not been hurt. How careless I was to allow myself to get hurt. Because of my accident I will still have another week before my time is up, for surely the master will require me to put in my full time. Yet what is one more week compared to the joy of being with my Martha again," he thought.

"Omne," said Philemon the next morning as the slave was starting out for work.

Omne jumped as he had not heard his master come up.

"Omne, you have done well. Your work has even been better than before. You did it well and never did you complain. The more work we gave you, the better you did it.

Even when badly injured you did not slow down for long. Last night your time was up. Report to the verandah of my house this afternoon, just before the evening meal. I will then tell you what will be ahead for you. You will work until half way between the noon meal and the evening meal. When it is time Seth will come to get you. At that time you will have a little free time. Go to the river and bathe, change into clean clothes and when it is time we will send for you."

"But sir, I missed 7 whole days of work. I have to make them up."

Philemon just smiled at the young man and said, "It is as I said." Then he turned and walked away.

The work seemed easy for Omne that day. Scarcely had he had his noon meal than it was time to stop work. How good the plunge in the cool water felt. He even had time to trim his beard and hair. He wanted to look as good as he felt. He still had some idle time after he was all dressed in clean clothes. "Father," he prayed, "Be my guide. Continue to bless me and to lead me.

As you have in the past, give me the strength to face what is ahead of me. Thy will be done." Then he heard a voice at his door calling for him. His heart beat fast as he went to meet her. Martha was standing there, radiant in smiles. We have a few minutes still. Let's go for a walk down to the stream. Walking hand in hand they drew near the water, sitting down in the shade of a tree.

It was so sweet just to be with each other and few words were spoken. Each savored this time together.

It seemed only moments, sitting there together, before it was time to go. Slowly they arose from the ground and headed for the master's house and to their future. She started to falter, but he gently held her to him for a moment, and then they continued on their way.

Nearing the house they could smell roasting meat and other good aromas.

"Martha, do you know what these good smells mean? Is the master giving a feast for someone?"

"It does seem like he is," she said quietly to him.

Seth met them and together they proceeded to the verandah. The master and Apphia were there already and also Tychicus.

"Tychicus," Omne said, "How good to see you." His eyes said what his mouth could not utter.

Philemon bade them sit down on the cushions provided for them. It was cool there, shaded from the late afternoon sun, secluded so it seemed from the rest of the world.

Seth stood while the others sat. He looked from one expectant face to another, taking time to gaze at each face, looking each in the eyes as if searching to their very souls.

Omne, on looking at Seth wondered to himself, "Has it been that long since I rescued that little boy? He is no longer a small boy but a strong, wise man." He studied the sturdy features of the young man standing before him.

Seth, catching Omne's eyes, gave Omne a friendly smile. Finally, after a nod from his father, he turned to Omne. "Omne, will you please stand for your verdict?"

Just then there was a commotion coming from out in front of the master's house. Voices were talking; someone wanted to be admitted to the group.

Tychicus slipped quietly out but returned in only a moment. "Sir, can I have a moment with you?"

Philemon and Tychicus stepped aside and whispered together for a few minutes. Then returning, Philemon said, "before you speak, my son, we have two more guests who I feel should be in here to hear the verdict. Tychicus is going to bring them in.

All eyes turned to watch to see who was important enough to be allowed admittance. They did not have to wait long.

"Simon! Thomas!" How did you get here?" Forgetting where he was and what was going to happen Omne jumped up and ran to greet his friends. "How did you know?"

"I saw them when I was at the sea shore several weeks ago," answered Tychicus. "But I am also surprised to see them here."

"We just had to come," said Thomas. After all this man," and he gave Omne another hug, "after all he has done for me I just had to come and see him."

"I feel the same," spoke up Simon. Omne has done a lot to help even me."

"Now shall we begin?" asked Philemon. Then turning to his son he said, "please continue."

"Omne, will you come up here?"

All eyes looked at Omne as he stood there, tall and straight.

"Omne because of your great love for us, your devotion to duty and willingness to help your master at whatever the cost, I give you this verdict." He paused as if savoring the suspense that hung in the air. "Long ago you showed your courage and love for us all by saving my life. I will be grateful to you forever. Long have you worked hard for us. Yes, you hurt us greatly when you left here but that is all behind now and you are now a changed man. You have worked seemingly beyond your strength these last 90 days. You did more even than was required of you. Yes, don't look surprised, we saw the extra work that you did. We noted your concern for the others you worked with, often doing part of their work when they were feeling too ill to do all their own work. One day you even did another man's full day's work, along with your own, working late and cutting deep into your short rest time, because he could not work at all that day. Yes, we know all about this and more.

Now because of your great devotion to my father and to me I am now setting you free. You are no longer a slave but a free man. Wait that is not all. You will be a brother to me, sharing completely with me in my father's inheritance.

My father is no longer your master. He is now a father to you." Here Seth reached to embrace Omne, but Omne was not there. Omne was kneeling at the feet of Philemon.

"Sir, do not tease me. Please..." But his speech was cut short.

"Omne, stand up. Do not kneel before me. I am but a man. Everything Seth says is true. You are my son, a very worthy son at that. Now do you know what else this means." Here he paused to look at Martha. "Martha, will you please come up here and stand next to Omne. As my son's wife, Martha is also free. Thus all of your children are also free."

At this both Omne and Martha fell to the ground, as in shock. Gently Seth and his father gathered them up and held them while the certainty of the good news sank in. When at last Omne and Martha could believe, Omne turned to Tychicus, now standing nearby.

"Yes," Tychicus answered to Omne's unspoken question, "It is all true. I am told that this was planned over a year ago, but they had to wait for you.

Turning again to Philemon Omne simply said, "thank you sir, I mean father. I will not let you down again. I will be worthy of your great love and trust in me."

Turning to Seth he said, "thank you for sharing with me your father."

Then he turned to Seth's mother. "And now you are my mother too. I feel you had a lot to do with this. I thank you for your love and trust in me even when I betrayed this trust. I will not betray your trust again. The LORD be my Judge in this."

Martha put her arms around her mistress and whispered, "Is it really true? Do I at last have a mother and a father? Oh what joy I will have as I work for you now."

"Work for me? You will no longer work for me."

For a moment a horrified look crossed Martha's face as these words hit her. "No longer work for you. Why I have to."

Gently the older woman took Martha in her arms. "Shall my daughter have to work for me day after day? What kind of a mother would I be to make my own daughter work like a servant?"

Martha stood back and looked long at the older woman. "But if I don't work for you whatever will I do all day long?"

Taking her hands in hers, Martha's new mother said, "You will find plenty to fill your days. You will see."

"Okay mother," replied Martha, with a tearful smile playing across her face, "if that is what you want. But it will take a lot of getting used to for me to remember this." She smiled at her new parents and noted their pleased expressions on their faces.

Then Martha remembered the past several weeks. The mistress had a young girl named Sarah helping Martha. At first Martha was worried that she was not doing her work well enough. Now the light came to her. "Mother, is that why you had Sarah working with me?"

"That is correct. I needed someone who could do the work that you have been doing for these many years. I think you have trained her well too. You are indeed a worthy daughter, a most loved daughter, one I have always wanted," spoke her new mother.

While they were talking Omne saw the other slaves come into the courtyard, each clean and wearing a broad smile on their face. Jethro walked up to Omne and said, "You deserve all the good the master has said. Even in my disappointment, I am glad you are back home," and his eyes shown his pleasure.

Martha came up as the two men were talking. "You are not mad at me anymore?" she asked.

"No I am not mad. Of course I am disappointed that I can not marry you but I am satisfied that you have with you a better man then I. I will continue doing my best for the master, as I have seen Omne' doing. You deserve that man," and he gave Martha a broad smile.

"Let the feast begin," said Philemon.

But Seth held up his hand. "One moment please. There are others here who wish to see Omne first, before we eat." Beckoning to a servant he waited a moment. "Here they are Omne."

Omne was surprised to see his brother David coming behind the servant. But who was that with him. There an older man and woman, both with silver hair. They walked towards Omne with hands outstretched. Nearing him David spoke, "Omnesimus greet your father and mother."

ABOUT THE AUTHOR

The author first did some writing when he helped with his school paper in high school. But it was only years later when failing eyesight caused him to retire early that he thought of writing.

He took a course from Hadley School for the Blind in Creative writing.

After buying his first computer his writing became easier and his short stories keep encouraging others. Some of these were written just because someone asked for a certain story.

Today he and his wife, Dorothy live just out of Walla Walla, WA where he continues to raise chickens and to grow a large garden.

Printed in the United States
19201LVS00008B/7-93